Stellar Acclaim

The Inhuman Condition

"Ever since the heyday of horror fiction . . . aficionados have been awaiting a writer to transcend the genre and give it new legitimacy. Clive Barker may be the man. He is as morbid as Stephen King, but unlike his American counterpart, this 33-year-old writer from Liverpool is witty, unpredictable and concise. . . . Each story involves an uncanny mix of eroticism and terror. . . . BARKER, ALREADY CELEBRATED IN BRITAIN, IS ABOUT TO SURFACE IN THE U.S. WITH DEMONIC FORCE."

—<u>Time</u>

"Barker create(s) an atmosphere of dread and foreboding. . . . What he adds . . . is a wicked willingness to use vivid images of violence to provide a jolt of R-rated realism to his fiction. . . . He makes a bad dream seem not only creepily disturbing but plausible. . . . <u>THE INHUMAN CONDITION</u> IS CLIVE BARKER AT HIS MOST EFFECTIVE."

—<u>The New York Times</u>

"Barker is providing plenty of explicit terror. . . . Clive Barker even scares Stephen King. . . . King says that some of the stories are 'so creepily awful that I literally could not read them alone. . . .'"

—<u>USA Today</u>

"REFRESHING CREATIVITY AND IMAGINATION . . . CLIVE BARKER'S TALES OF TERROR ARE AS PROVOCATIVE AS THEY ARE FUN TO READ."

—<u>Baltimore Sun</u>

Books by Clive Barker

In the Flesh
The Inhuman Condition
Weaveworld

Published by POCKET BOOKS

Most Pocket Books are available at special quantity discounts for bulk purchases for sales promotions, premiums or fund raising. Special books or book excerpts can also be created to fit specific needs.

For details write the office of the Vice President of Special Markets, Pocket Books, 1230 Avenue of the Americas, New York, New York 10020.

TALES OF TERROR BY

CLIVE BARKER

THE INHUMAN CONDITION

POCKET BOOKS

New York   London   Toronto   Sydney   Tokyo

POCKET BOOKS, a division of Simon & Schuster Inc.
1230 Avenue of the Americas, New York, NY 10020

Copyright © 1985 by Clive Barker
Cover art © 1987 Jim Warren

Originally published in Great Britain by Sphere Books Ltd.
under the title *Books of Blood, Volume IV*. Published in hardcover
in the United States by Poseidon Press.
Published by arrangement with the author.
Library of Congress Catalog Number: 86-5086

ISBN: 0-671-68463-9

First Pocket Books printing August 1987

10 9 8 7 6 5 4

POCKET and colophon are trademarks of
Simon & Schuster Inc.

Printed in the U.S.A.

To Alec and Con

Acknowledgments

My thanks to: Doug Bennett, who got me into Pentonville—and out again—in the same day, and later furnished me with his insights on prisons and the prison service; to Jim Burr, for his mind's eye tour of White Deer, Texas, and for the New York adventures; to Ros Stanwell-Smith, for her enthusiastic detailing of plagues and how to start them; and to Barbara Boote, my tireless editor, whose enthusiasm has proved the best possible spur to invention.

Contents

The
Inhuman
Condition

ARE you the one then?" Red demanded, seizing hold of the derelict by the shoulder of his squalid gabardine.

"What one d'you mean?" the dirt-caked face replied. He was scanning the quartet of young men who'd cornered him with rodent's eyes. The tunnel where they'd found him relieving himself was far from hope of help. They all knew it and so, it seemed, did he. "I don't know what you're talking about."

"You've been showing yourself to children," Red said.

The man shook his head, a dribble of spittle running from his lip into the matted bush of his beard. "I've done nothing," he insisted.

Brendan sauntered across to the man, heavy footsteps hollow in the tunnel. "What's your name?" he inquired, with deceptive courtesy. Though he lacked Red's height and commanding manner, the scar that inscribed Brendan's cheek from temple to jawline suggested he knew suffering, both in the giving and the receiving. *"Name,"* he demanded. "I'm not going to ask you again."

"Pope," the old man muttered. "Mr. Pope."

Brendan grinned. *"Mr.* Pope?" he said. "Well, we heard you've been exposing that rancid little prick of yours to innocent children. What do you say to that?"

"No," Pope replied, again shaking his head. "That's not true. I never done nothing like that." When he frowned the filth on his face cracked like crazy paving, a second skin of grime which was the accrual of many months. Had it not been for the fragrance of alcohol off him, which obscured the worst of his bodily stench, it would have been nigh on impossible to stand within a yard of him. The man was human refuse, a shame to his species.

"Why bother with him?" Karney said. "He stinks."

Red glanced over his shoulder to silence the interruption. At seventeen, Karney was the youngest, and in the quartet's unspoken hierarchy scarcely deserving of an opinion. Recognizing his error, he shut up, leaving Red to return his attention to the vagrant. He pushed Pope back against the wall of the tunnel. The old man expelled a cry as he struck the concrete; it echoed back and forth. Karney, knowing from past experience how the scene would go from here, moved away and studied a gilded cloud of gnats on the edge of the tunnel. Though he enjoyed being with Red and the other two— the camaraderie, the petty larceny, the drinking—this particular game had never been much to his taste. He couldn't see the sport in finding some drunken wreck of a man like Pope and beating what little sense was left in his deranged head out of him. It made Karney feel dirty, and he wanted no part of it.

Red pulled Pope off the wall and spat a stream of abuse into the man's face, then, when he failed to get an adequate response, threw him back against the tunnel a second time, more forcibly than the first, following through by taking the breathless man by both lapels and shaking him until he rattled. Pope threw a panicky glance up and down the track. A railway had once run along this route through Highgate and Finsbury Park. The track was long gone, however, and the site was public parkland, popular with early morning joggers and late-evening lovers. Now, in the middle of a clammy afternoon, the track was deserted in both directions.

"Hey," said Catso, "don't break his bottles."

"Right," said Brendan, "we should dig out the drink before we break his head."

At the mention of being robbed of his liquor Pope began to struggle, but his thrashing only served to enrage his captor. Red was in a dirty mood. The day, like most days this Indian summer, had been sticky and dull. Only the dog-end of a wasted season to endure; nothing to do, and no money to spend. Some entertainment had been called for, and it had fallen to Red as lion, and Pope as Christian, to supply it.

"You'll get hurt if you struggle," Red advised the man, "we only want to see what you've got in your pockets."

"None of your business," Pope retorted, and for a moment he spoke as a man who had once been used to being obeyed. The outburst made Karney turn from the gnats and gaze at Pope's emaciated face. Nameless degeneracies had drained it of dignity or vigor, but something remained there, glimmering beneath the dirt. What had the man been, Karney wondered? A banker perhaps? A judge, now lost to the law forever?

Catso had now stepped into the fray to search Pope's clothes, while Red held his prisoner against the tunnel wall by the throat. Pope fought off Catso's unwelcome attentions as best he could, his arms flailing like windmills, his eyes getting progressively wilder. Don't fight, Karney willed him, it'll be worse for you if you do. But the old man seemed to be on the verge of panic. He was letting out small grunts of protest that were more animal than human.

"Somebody hold his arms," Catso said, ducking beneath Pope's attack. Brendan grabbed hold of Pope's wrists and wrenched the man's arms up above his head to facilitate an easier search. Even now, with any hope of release dashed, Pope continued to squirm. He managed to land a solid kick to Red's left shin, for which he received a blow in return. Blood broke from his nose and ran down into his mouth. There was more color where that came from, Karney knew. He'd seen pictures aplenty of spilled people—bright, gleaming coils of guts; yellow fat and purple lungs—all that brilliance was locked up in the gray sack of Pope's body. Why such a thought should occur to him Karney wasn't certain. It distressed him, and he tried to turn his attention back to the gnats, but Pope demanded his attention, loosing a cry of anguish as Catso ripped open one of his several waistcoats to get to the lower layers.

"*Bastards!*" Pope screeched, not seeming to care that his insults would inevitably earn him further blows. "Take your shitting hands off me or I'll have you *dead*. All of you!" Red's fist brought an end to the threats, and

16

blood came running after blood. Pope spat it back at his tormentor. "Don't tempt me," Pope said, his voice dropping to a murmur. "I warn you . . ."

"You smell like a dead dog," Brendan said. "Is that what you are: a dead dog?"

Pope didn't grant him a reply. His eyes were on Catso, who was systematically emptying the coat and waistcoat pockets and tossing a pathetic collection of keepsakes into the dust on the tunnel floor.

"Karney," Red snapped, "look through the stuff, will you? See if there's anything worth having."

Karney stared at the plastic trinkets and the soiled ribbons, at the tattered sheets of paper (was the man a poet?) and the wine-bottle corks. "It's all trash," he said.

"Look anyway," Red instructed. "Could be money wrapped in that stuff." Karney made no move to comply. "*Look,* damn you."

Reluctantly, Karney went down on his haunches and proceeded to sift through the mound of rubbish Catso was still depositing in the dirt. He could see at a glance that there was nothing of value there, though perhaps some of the items—the battered photographs, the all but indecipherable notes—might offer some clue to the man Pope had been before drink and incipient lunacy had driven the memories away. Curious as he was, Karney wished to respect Pope's privacy. It was all the man had left.

"There's nothing here," he announced after a cursory examination. But Catso hadn't finished his search. The deeper he dug the more layers of filthy clothing presented themselves to his eager hands. Pope had more pockets than a master magician.

Karney glanced up from the forlorn heap of belongings and found, to his discomfort, that Pope's eyes were on him. The old man, exhausted and beaten, had given up his protests. He looked pitiful. Karney opened his hands to signify that he had taken nothing from the heap. Pope, by way of reply, offered a tiny nod.

"Got it!" Catso yelled triumphantly. "Got the fucker!" and pulled a bottle of vodka from one of the pockets. Pope was either too feeble to notice that his alcohol supply had been snatched or too tired to care. Whichever way, he made no sound of complaint as the liquor was stolen from him.

"Any more?" Brendan wanted to know. He'd begun to giggle, a high-pitched laugh that signaled his escalating excitement. "Maybe the dog's got more where that came from," he said, letting Pope's hands fall and pushing Catso aside. The latter made no objection to the treatment. He had his bottle and was satisfied. He smashed off the neck to avoid contamination and began to drink, squatting in the dirt. Red relinquished his grip on Pope now that Brendan had taken charge. He was clearly bored with the game. Brendan, on the other hand, was just beginning to get a taste for it.

Red walked over to Karney and turned over the pile of Pope's belongings with the toe of his boot.

"Fucking wash-out," he stated, without feeling.

"Yeah," Karney said, hoping that Red's disaffection would signal an end to the old man's humiliation. But Red had thrown the bone to Brendan, and he knew better than to try and snatch it back. Karney had seen Brendan's capacity for violence before and he had no desire to watch the man at work again. Sighing, he stood up and turned his back on Brendan's activities. The echoes off the tunnel's wall were all too eloquent however, a mingling of punches and breathless obscenities. On past evidence nothing would stop Brendan until his fury was spent. Anyone foolish enough to interrupt him would find themselves victims in their turn.

Red had sauntered across to the far side of the tunnel, lit a cigarette, and was watching the punishment meted out with casual interest. Karney glanced around at Catso. He had descended from squatting to sitting in the dirt, the bottle of vodka between his outstretched legs. He was grinning to himself, deaf to the drool of pleas falling from Pope's broken mouth.

Karney felt sick to his stomach. More to divert his attention from the beating than out of genuine interest, he returned to the junk filched from Pope's pockets and turned it over, picking up one of the photographs to examine. It was of a child, though it was impossible to make any guess as to family resemblance. Pope's face was now barely recognizable; one eye had already begun to close as the bruise around it swelled. Karney tossed the photograph back with the rest of the mementoes. As he did so he caught sight of a length of knotted cord which he had previously passed over. He glanced back up at Pope. The puffed eye was closed, the other seemed sightless. Satisfied that he wasn't being watched, Karney pulled the string from where it lay, coiled like a snake in its nest, among the trash. Knots fascinated him and always had. Though he had never possessed skill with academic puzzles (mathematics was a mystery to him; the intricacies of language the same) he had always had a taste for more tangible riddles.

Given a knot, a jigsaw or a railway timetable, he was happily lost to himself for hours. The interest went back to his childhood, which had been solitary. With neither father nor siblings to engage his attention what better companion than a puzzle?

He turned the string over and over, examining the three knots set at inch intervals in the middle of its length. They were large and asymmetrical and seemed to serve no discernible purpose except, perhaps, to infatuate minds like his own. How else to explain their cunning construction except that the knotter had been at pains to create a problem that was well nigh insoluble? He let his fingers play over the surfaces of the knots, instinctively seeking some latitude, but they had been so brilliantly contrived that no needle, however fine, could have been pushed between the intersected strands. The challenge they presented was too appealing to ignore. Again he glanced up at the old man. Brendan had apparently tired of his labors. As Karney looked on he threw the old man against the tunnel wall and let the body sink to the ground. Once there, he let it lie. An unmistakable sewer stench rose from it.

"That was good," Brendan pronounced like a man who had stepped from an invigorating shower. The exercise had raised a sheen of sweat on his ruddy features; he was smiling from ear to ear. "Give me some of that vodka, Catso."

"All gone," Catso slurred, upending the bottle. "Wasn't more than a throatful in it."

"You're a lying shit," Brendan told him, still grinning.

"What if I am?" Catso replied, and tossed the empty

bottle away. It smashed. "Help me up," he requested of Brendan. The latter, his great good humor intact, helped Catso to his feet. Red had already started to walk out of the tunnel; the others followed.

"Hey Karney," Catso said over his shoulder, "you coming?"

"Sure."

"You want to kiss the dog better?" Brendan suggested. Catso was almost sick with laughter at the remark. Karney made no answer. He stood up, his eyes glued to the inert figure slumped on the tunnel floor, watching for a flicker of consciousness. There was none that he could see. He glanced after the others. All three had their backs to him as they made their way down the track. Swiftly, Karney pocketed the knots. The theft took moments only. Once the cord was safely out of sight he felt a surge of triumph which was out of all proportion to the goods he'd gained. He was already anticipating the hours of amusement the knots would furnish. Time when he could forget himself, and his emptiness; forget the sterile summer and the loveless winter ahead; forget too the old man lying in his own waste yards from where he stood.

"Karney!" Catso called.

Karney turned his back on Pope and began to walk away from the body and the attendant litter of belongings. A few paces from the edge of the tunnel the old man behind him began to mutter in his delirium. The words were incomprehensible. But by some acoustic trick, the walls of the tunnel multiplied the sound. Pope's voice was thrown back and forth and back again, filling the tunnel with whispers.

* * *

It wasn't until much later that night, when he was sitting alone in his bedroom with his mother weeping in her sleep next door, that Karney had the opportunity to study the knots at leisure. He had said nothing to Red or the others about his stealing the cord. The theft was so minor they would have mocked him for mentioning it. And besides, the knots offered him a personal challenge, one which he would face—and conceivably fail—in private.

After some debate with himself he elected the knot he would first attempt and began to work at it. Almost immediately he lost all sense of time passing; the problem engrossed him utterly. Hours of blissful frustration passed unnoticed as he analyzed the tangle, looking for some clue as to a hidden system in the knotting. He could find none. The configurations, if they *had* some rationale, were beyond him. All he could hope to do was tackle the problem by trial and error. Dawn was threatening to bring the world to light again when he finally relinquished the cord to snatch a few hours of sleep, and in a night's work he had merely managed to loosen a tiny fraction of the knot.

Over the next four days the problem became an *idée fixe*, a hermetic obsession to which he would return at any available opportunity, picking at the knot with fingers that were increasingly numb with use. The puzzle enthralled him as little in his adult life ever had. Working at the knot he was deaf and blind to the outside world. Sitting in his lamp-lit room by night, or in the park by day, he could almost feel himself drawn into its snarled heart, his consciousness focused so minutely it could go where light could not. But despite his persistence, the unraveling proved a slow business. Unlike most knots he had encountered, which, once loosened in part, conceded the entire solution, this structure was so adroitly designed that prising one element loose only served to constrict and tighten another. The trick, he began to grasp, was to work on all sides of the knot at an equal rate, loosening one part a fraction then moving around to loosen another to an equal degree, and so on. This systematic rotation, though tedious, gradually showed results.

He saw nothing of Red, Brendan or Catso in this time. Their silence suggested that they mourned his absence as little as he mourned theirs. He was surprised, therefore, when Catso turned up looking for him on Friday evening. He had come with a proposal. He and Brendan had found a house ripe for robbery and wanted Karney as lookout man. He had fulfilled that role twice in the past. Both had been small breaking and entering jobs like this, which on the first occasion had netted a number of salable items of jewelry, and on the second several hundred pounds in cash. This time, however, the job was to be done without Red's involvement. He was increasingly taken up with Anelisa, and she, according to Catso, had made him swear off petty theft and save his talents for something more ambitious. Karney sensed that Catso—and Brendan too, most likely—was itching to prove his criminal proficiency without Red. The house they had chosen was an easy target, so Catso claimed, and Karney would be a damn fool to let a chance of such easy pickings pass by. He nodded along with Catso's enthusiasm, his mind on other pickings. When Catso finally finished his spiel Karney agreed to the job, not for the money, but because saying yes would get him back to the knot soonest.

Much later that evening, at Catso's suggestion, they met to look at the site of the proposed job. The location certainly suggested an easy take. Karney had often walked over the bridge that carried Hornsey Lane across the Archway Road, but he had never noticed the steep footpath—part steps, part track—that ran from the side of the bridge down to the road below. Its entrance was narrow and easily overlooked, and its meandering length was lit by only one lamp, which light was obscured by trees growing in the gardens that backed on to the pathway. It was these gardens—their back fences easily scaled or wrenched down—that offered such perfect access to the houses. A thief, using the secluded footpath, might come and go with impunity, unseen by travelers on either the road above or that below. All the setup required was a lookout on the pathway to warn of the occasional pedestrian who might use the footpath. This would be Karney's duty.

The following night was a thief's joy. Cool, but not cold; cloudy, but without rain. They met on Highgate Hill, at the gates of the Church of the Passionist Fathers, and from there made their way down to the Archway Road. Approaching the pathway from the top end would, Brendan had argued, attract more attention. Police patrols were more common on Hornsey Lane, in part because the bridge was irresistible to local depressives. For the committed suicide the venue had distinct advantages, its chief appeal being that if the eighty-foot drop didn't kill you the juggernauts hurtling south on the Archway Road certainly would.

thing that had lifted him up to meet its slitted and chancred face. Now, as he reached the Archway Road, he felt tremors beginning in his limbs. If his legs gave out he was certain it would come for him again and lay its mouth on his as it already had. Only this time he would not have the strength to scream; the life would be sucked from his lungs. His only hope lay in putting the road between him and his tormentor. The beast's breath loud in his ears, he scaled the crash barrier, leaped down to the road, and began across the southbound freeway at a run. Halfway across he realized his error. The horror in his head had blinded him to all other risks. A blue Volvo — its driver's mouth a perfect O — bore down on him. He was caught in its headlights like an animal, entranced. Two instants later he was struck a glancing blow which threw him across the divide and into the path of a tractor trailer. The second driver had no chance to swerve. The impact split Catso open and tossed him beneath the wheels.

Up in the garden, Karney heard the panic of the brakes and the policeman at the bottom of the pathway say: "Jesus Christ Almighty." He waited a few seconds, then peered out from his hiding place. The footpath was now deserted, top to bottom. The trees were quite still. From the road below rose the sound of a siren, and that of the officers shouting for oncoming cars to halt. Closer by, somebody was sobbing. He listened intently for a few moments, trying to work out the source of the sobs, before realizing that they were his own. Tears or no, the clamor from below demanded his attention. Something terrible had happened, and he had to see what. But he was afraid to run the gauntlet of the trees, knowing what lay in wait there, so he stood, staring up into the branches, trying to locate the beast. There was neither sound nor movement, however. The trees were dead still. Stifling his fears, he climbed from his hiding place and began to walk down the pathway, his eyes glued to the foliage for the slightest sign of the beast's presence. He could hear the buzz of a gathering crowd. The thought of a press of people comforted him. From now on he would need a place to hide, wouldn't he? Men who'd seen miracles did.

He had reached the spot where Catso had been dragged up into the trees; a litter of leaves and stolen property marked it. Karney's feet wanted to be swift, to pick him up and whisk him away from the place, but some perverse instinct slowed his pace. Was it that he wanted to tempt the knot's child into showing its face? Better, perhaps, to confront it now—in all its foulness —than to live in fear from this moment on, embroidering its countenance and its capacities. But the beast kept itself hidden. If indeed it was still up there in the tree, it twitched not a nail.

Something moved beneath his foot. Karney looked down, and there, almost lost among the leaves, was the cord. Catso had been deemed unworthy to carry it apparently. Now—with some clue to its power revealed —it made no effort to pass for natural. It squirmed on the gravel like a serpent in heat, rearing its knotted head to attract Karney's attention. He wanted to ignore its cavorting but he couldn't. He knew that if *he* didn't pick up the knots somebody else would, given time; a victim, like himself, of an urge to solve enigmas. Where could such innocence lead, except to another escape perhaps more terrible than the first? No, it was best that he took the knots. At least he was alive to their potential, and so, in part, armored against it. He bent down, and as he did so the string fairly leaped into his hands, wrapping itself around his fingers so tightly he almost cried out.

"Bastard," he said.

The string coiled itself around his hand, weaving its length between his fingers in an ecstasy of welcome. He raised his hand to watch its performance better. His concern for the events on the Archway Road had suddenly, almost miraculously, evaporated. What did such petty concerns matter? It was only life and death. Better to make his getaway now, while he could.

Above his head a branch shook. He unglued his eyes from the knots and squinted up into the tree. With the cord restored to him his trepidation, like his fears, had evaporated.

"Show yourself," he said. "I'm not like Catso; I'm not afraid. I want to know what you are."

From its camouflage of leaves the waiting beast leaned down toward Karney and exhaled a single, chilly breath. It smelled of the river at low tide, of vegetation gone to rot. Karney was about to ask it what it was again when he realized that the exhalation *was* the beast's reply. All it could speak of its condition was contained in that bitter and rancid breath. As replies went, it was not lacking in eloquence. Distressed by the images it awoke, Karney backed away from the spot. Wounded, sluggish forms moved behind his eyes, engulfed in a sludge of filth.

A few feet from the tree the spell of the breath broke, and Karney drank the polluted air from the road as though it were clean as the world's morning. He turned his back on the agonies he had sensed, thrust his string-woven hand into his pocket, and began up the pathway. Behind him, the trees were quite still again.

Several dozen spectators had gathered on the bridge to watch the proceedings below. Their presence had in turn piqued the curiosity of drivers making their way along Hornsey Lane, some of whom had parked their vehicles and gotten out to join the throng. The scene beneath the bridge seemed too remote to wake any feelings in Karney. He stood among the chattering crowd and gazed down quite dispassionately. He recognized Catso's corpse from his clothes; little else remained of his sometime companion.

In a while, he knew, he would have to mourn. But at present he could feel nothing. After all, Catso was dead, wasn't he? His pain and confusion were at an end. Karney sensed he would be wiser to save his tears for those whose agonies were only just beginning.

And again, the knots.

At home that night he tried to put them away, but, after the events of the evening they had taken on a fresh glamour. *The knots bound beasts*. How, and why, he couldn't know; nor, curiously, did he much care at the moment. All his life he had accepted that the world was rich with mysteries a mind of his limited grasp had no hope of understanding. That was the only genuine lesson his schooldays had taught: that he was ignorant. This new imponderable was just another to tag onto a long list.

Only one rationale really occurred to him, and that was that somehow Pope had arranged his stealing of the knots in the full knowledge that the loosened beast would revenge itself on the old man's tormentors; and it wasn't to be until Catso's cremation, six days later, that Karney was to get some confirmation of that theory. In the interim he kept his fears to himself, reasoning that the less he said about the night's events the less harm they could do him. Talk lent the fantastic credibility. It gave weight to phenomena which he hoped, if left to themselves, would become too frail to survive.

When the following day the police came to the house on a routine questioning of Catso's friends, he claimed he knew nothing of the circumstances surrounding the death. Brendan had done the same, and as there had seemingly been no witnesses to offer contrary testimony, Karney was not questioned again. Instead he was left to his thoughts; and the knots.

Once, he saw Brendan. He had expected recriminations. Brendan's belief was that Catso had been running from the police when he was killed, and it had been Karney's lack of concentration that had failed to alert them to the Law's proximity. But Brendan made no accusations. He had taken the burden of guilt onto himself with a willingness that almost smacked of appetite; he spoke only of his own failure, not of Karney's. The apparent arbitrariness of Catso's demise had uncovered an unexpected tenderness in Brendan, and Karney ached to tell him the whole incredible story from beginning to end. But this was not the time, he sensed. He let Brendan spill his hurt out, and kept his own mouth shut.

And still the knots.

Sometimes he would wake in the middle of the night and feel the cord moving beneath his pillow. Its presence was comforting, its eagerness was not, waking, as it did, a similar eagerness in him. He wanted to touch the remaining knots and examine the puzzles they offered. But he knew that to do so was tempting capitulation: to his own fascination, to their hunger for release. When such temptation arose, he forced himself to remember the pathway, and the beast in the trees; to awake again the harrowing thoughts that had come with the beast's breath. Then, by degrees, remembered distress would cancel present curiosity, and he would leave the cord where it lay. Out of sight, though seldom out of mind.

Dangerous as he knew the knots to be, he couldn't bring himself to burn them. As long as he possessed that modest length of cord he was unique. To relinquish it would be to return to his hitherto nondescript condition. He was not willing to do that, even though he suspected that his daily and intimate association with the cord was systematically weakening his ability to resist its seduction.

Of the thing in the tree he saw nothing. He even began to wonder if he hadn't imagined the whole confrontation. Indeed, given time, his powers to rationalize the truth into nonexistence might have won the day completely. But events subsequent to the cremation of Catso put an end to such a convenient option.

Karney had gone to the service alone—and, despite the presence of Brendan, Red and Anelisa—he had left alone. He had little wish to speak with any of the mourners. Whatever words he might once have had to frame the events were becoming more difficult to reinvent as time passed. He hurried away from the crematorium before anyone could approach him to talk, his head bowed against the dusty wind which had brought periods of cloud and bright sunshine in swift succession throughout the day. As he walked, he dug in his pocket for a pack of cigarettes. The cord, waiting there as ever, welcomed his fingers in its usual ingratiating manner. He disentangled it and took out the cigarettes, but the wind was too snappy for matches to stay alight, and his hands seemed unable to perform the simple task of masking the flame. He wandered on a little way until he found an alley and stepped into it to light up. Pope was there, waiting for him.

"Did you send flowers?" the derelict asked.

Karney's instinct was to turn and run. But the sunlit road was no more than yards away; he was in no danger here. And an exchange with the old man might prove informative.

"No flowers?" Pope said.

"No flowers," Karney returned. "What are you doing here?"

"Same as you," Pope replied. "Came to see the boy burn." He grinned; the expression on that wretched, grimy face was repulsive to a fault. Pope was still the bag of bones that he'd been in the tunnel two weeks previously, but now an air of threat hung about him. Karney was grateful to have the sun at his back.

"And you. To see you," Pope said.

Karney chose to make no reply. He struck a match and lit his cigarette.

"You've got something that belongs to me," Pope said. Karney volunteered no guilt. "I want my knots back, boy, before you do some *real* damage."

"I don't know what you're talking about," Karney replied. His gaze concentrated, unwillingly, on Pope's face, drawn into its intricacies. The alleyway, with its piled refuse, twitched. A cloud had apparently drifted over the sun, for Karney's vision, but for the figure of Pope, darkened subtly.

"It was stupid, boy, to try and steal from me. Not that I wasn't easy prey. That was my error and it won't happen again. I get lonely sometimes, you see. I'm sure you understand. And when I'm lonely I take to drinking."

Though mere seconds had apparently passed since Karney had lit his cigarette, it had burned down to the filter without his taking a single pull on it. He dropped it, vaguely aware that time, as well as space, was being pulled out of true in the tiny passage.

"It wasn't me," he muttered; a child's defense in the face of any and every accusation.

"Yes it was," Pope replied with incontestable authority. "Let's not waste breath with fabrication. You stole from me, and your colleague has paid the price. You can't undo the harm you've done. But you *can* prevent further harm, if you return to me what's mine. *Now.*"

Karney's hand had strayed to his pocket, without his quite realizing it. He wanted to get out of this trap before it snapped on him. Giving Pope what was, after all, rightfully *his* was surely the easiest way to do it. His fingers hesitated, however. Why? Because the Methuselah's eyes were so implacable perhaps; because returning the knots into Pope's hands gave him total control over the weapon that had, in effect, killed Catso? But more, even now, with sanity at risk, Karney was loath to give back the only fragment of mystery that had ever come his way. Pope, sensing his disinclination, pressed his cajoling into a higher gear.

"Don't be afraid of me," he said. "I won't do you any harm unless you push me to it. I would *much* prefer that we concluded this matter peacefully. More violence, another death even, would only attract attention."

Is this a killer I'm looking at? Karney thought; so unkempt, so ridiculously feeble. And yet sound contradicted sight. The seed of command Karney had once heard in Pope's voice was now in full flower.

"Do you want money?" Pope asked. "Is that it? Would your pride be best appeased if I offered you something for your troubles?" Karney looked incredulously at Pope's shabbiness. "Oh," the old man said, "I may not look like a moneyed man, but appearances can be deceptive. In fact, that's the rule, not the exception. Take yourself, for instance. You don't look like a dead man, but take it from me, you are as good as dead, boy. I promise you death if you continue to defy me."

The speech—so measured, so scrupulous—startled Karney, coming as it did from Pope's lips. Two weeks ago they had caught Pope in his cups—confused and vulnerable—but now, sober, the man spoke like a potentate; a lunatic king, perhaps, going among the hoi polloi as a pauper. King? No, more like *priest*. Something in the nature of his authority (in his name, even) suggested a man whose power had never been rooted in mere politics.

"Once more," he said, "I request you to give me what's mine."

He took a step toward Karney. The alleyway was a narrow tunnel, pressing down on their heads. If there was sky above them, Pope had blinded it.

"Give me the knots," he said. His voice was softly reassuring. The darkness had closed in completely. All Karney could see was the man's mouth: his uneven teeth, his gray tongue. "Give them to me, thief, or suffer the consequences."

"Karney?"

Red's voice came from another world. It was just a few paces away—the voice, sunlight, wind—but for a long moment Karney struggled to locate it again.

"Karney?"

He dragged his consciousness out from between Pope's teeth and forced his face around to look at the road. Red was there, standing in the sun, Anelisa at his side. Her blond hair shone.

"What's going on?"

"Leave us alone," Pope said. "We've got business, he and I."

"You've got business with *him?*" Red asked of Karney.

Before Karney could reply Pope said: "Tell him. Tell him, Karney, you want to speak to me alone."

Red threw a glance over Karney's shoulder toward the old man. "You want to tell me what's going on?" he said.

Karney's tongue was laboring to find a response, but failing. The sunlight was so far away; every time a cloud-shadow passed across the street he feared the light would be extinguished permanently. His lips worked silently to express his fear.

"You all right?" Red asked. "*Karney?* Can you hear me?"

Karney nodded. The darkness that held him was beginning to lift.

"Yes . . ." he said.

Suddenly, Pope threw himself at Karney, his hands scrabbling desperately for his pockets. The impact of the attack carried Karney, still in a stupor, back against the wall of the alleyway. He fell sideways against a pile of crates. They, and he, toppled over, and Pope, his grip on Karney too fierce to be dislodged, fell too. All the preceding calm—the gallows humor, the circumspect threats—had evaporated. He was again the idiot dere-lict, spouting insanities. Karney felt the man's hands tearing at his clothes and raking his skin in his bid for the knots. The words he was shouting into Karney's face were no longer comprehensible.

Red stepped into the alley and attempted to drag the old man, by coat or hair or beard, whichever handhold presented itself, off his victim. It was easier said than done; the assault had all the fury of a fit. But Red's superior strength won out. Spitting nonsense, Pope was pulled to his feet. Red held on to him as if he were a mad dog.

"Get up . . ." he told Karney, "get out of his reach."

Karney staggered to his feet among the tinder of crates. In the scant seconds of his attack Pope had done considerable damage. Karney was bleeding in half a dozen places. His clothes had been savaged; his shirt ripped beyond repair. Tentatively, he put his hand to his raked face. The scratches were raised like ritual scars.

Red pushed Pope against the wall. The derelict was still apoplectic, eyes wild. A stream of invective—a jumble of English and gibberish—was flung in Red's face. Without pausing in his tirade Pope made another attempt to attack Karney, but this time Red's handhold prevented the claws from making contact. Red hauled Pope out of the alley and into the road.

"Your lip's bleeding," Anelisa said, looking at Kar-ney with plain disgust. Karney could taste the blood,

41

salty and hot. He put the back of his hand to his mouth. It came away scarlet.

"Good thing we came after you," she said.

"Yeah," he returned, not looking at the woman. He was ashamed of the showing he'd made in the face of the vagrant and knew she must be laughing at his inability to defend himself. Her family were villains to a man, her father a folk hero among thieves.

Red came back in from the street. Pope had gone.

"What was all that about?" he demanded to know, taking a comb from his jacket pocket and rearranging his hair.

"Nothing," Karney replied.

"Don't give me shit," Red said. "He claims you stole something from him. Is that right?"

Karney glanced across at Anelisa. But for her presence he might have been willing to tell Red everything, there and then. She returned his glance and seemed to read his thoughts. Shrugging, she moved out of earshot, kicking through the demolished crates as she went.

"He's got it in for us all, Red," Karney said.

"What are you talking about?"

Karney looked down at his bloody hand. Even with Anelisa out of the way, the words to explain what he suspected were slow in coming.

"Catso . . ." he began.

"What about him?"

"He was running, Red."

Behind him, Anelisa expelled an irritated sigh. This was taking longer than she had temper for.

"Red," she said, "we'll be late."

"Wait a minute," Red told her sharply and turned his

attention back to Karney. "What do you mean: about Catso?"

"The old man's not what he seems. He's not a vagrant."

"Oh? What is he?" A note of sarcasm had crept back into Red's voice, for Anelisa's benefit, no doubt. The girl had tired of descretion and had wandered back to join Red. "What is he, Karney?"

Karney shook his head. What was the use of trying to explain a *part* of what had happened? Either he attempted the entire story, or nothing at all. Silence was easier.

"It doesn't matter," he said flatly.

Red gave him a puzzled look, then, when there was no clarification forthcoming, said: "If you've got something to tell me about Catso, Karney, I'd like to hear it. You know where I live."

"Sure," said Karney.

"I mean it," Red said, "about talking."

"Thanks."

"Catso was a good mate, you know? Bit of a piss-artist, but we've all had our moments, eh? He shouldn't have died, Karney. It was wrong."

"Red—"

"She's calling you." Anelisa had wandered out into the street.

"She's always calling me. I'll see you around, Karney."

"Yeah."

Red patted Karney's stinging cheek and followed Anelisa out into the sun. Karney made no move to follow them. Pope's assault had left him trembling. He intended to wait in the alleyway until he'd regained a gloss of composure, at least. Seeking reassurance of the knots he put his hand into his jacket pocket. It was empty. He checked his other pockets. They too were empty, and yet he was certain that the old man's grasp had failed to get near the cord. Perhaps they had slipped out of hiding during the struggle. Karney began to scour the alley, and when the first search failed, followed with a second and a third. But by that time he knew the operation was lost. Pope *had* succeeded after all. By stealth or chance, he had regained the knots.

With startling clarity, Karney remembered standing on Suicides' Leap, looking down on to the Archway Road, Catso's body sprawled below at the center of a network of lights and vehicles. He had felt so *removed* from the tragedy, viewing it with all the involvement of a passing bird. Now—suddenly—he was shot from the sky. He was on the ground, and wounded, waiting hopelessly for the terrors to come. He tasted blood from his split lip and wondered, wishing the thought would vanish even as it formed, if Catso had died immediately, or if he too had tasted blood as he'd lain there on the tarmac looking up at the people on the bridge who had yet to learn how close death was.

He returned home via the most populated route he could plan. Though this exposed his disreputable state to the stares of matrons and policemen alike he preferred their disapproval to chancing the empty streets away from the major thoroughfares. Once home, he bathed his scratches and put on a fresh set of clothes, then sat in front of the television for a while to allow his limbs to stop shaking. It was late afternoon, and the programs were all children's fare; a tone of queasy optimism infected every channel. He watched the banalities with his eyes but not with his mind, using the respite to try and find the words to describe all that had happened to him. The imperative was now to warn Red and Brendan. With Pope in control of the knots it could only be a matter of time before some beast—worse, perhaps, than the thing in the trees—came looking for them all. Then it would be too late for explanations. He knew the other two would be contemptuous, but he would sweat to convince them, however ridiculous he ended up looking in the process. Perhaps his tears and his panic would move them the way his impoverished vocabulary never could. About five after five, before his mother returned home from work, he slipped out of the house and went to find Brendan.

Anelisa took the piece of string she'd found in the alleyway out of her pocket and examined it. Why she had bothered to pick it up at all she wasn't certain, but somehow it had found its way into her hand. She played with one of the knots, risking her long nails in doing so. She had half a dozen better things to be doing with her early evening. Red had gone to buy drink and cigarettes and she had promised herself a leisurely, scented bath before he returned. But the knot wouldn't take that long to untie, she was certain of that. Indeed, it seemed almost eager to be undone; she had the strangest sensation of movement in it. And more intriguing yet, there were colors in the knot—she could see glints of crimson and violet. Within a few minutes she had forgotten the bath entirely; it could wait. Instead, she concentrated on the conundrum at her fingertips. After only a few minutes she began to see the light.

* * *

Karney told Brendan the story as best he could. Once he had taken the plunge and begun it from the beginning he discovered it had its own momentum, which carried him through to the present tense with relatively little hesitation. He finished, saying: "I know it sounds wild, but it's all true."

Brendan didn't believe a word; that much was apparent in his blank stare. But there was more than disbelief on the scarred face. Karney couldn't work out what it was until Brendan took hold of his shirt. Only then did he see the depth of Brendan's fury.

"You don't think it's bad enough that Catso's dead," he seethed, "you have to come here telling me this shit."

"It's the truth."

"And where are these fucking knots now?"

"I told you, the old man's got them. He took them this afternoon. He's going to kill us, Bren. I know it."

Brendan let Karney go. "Tell you what I'm going to do," he said magnanimously. "I'm going to forget you told me any of this."

"You don't understand—"

"I *said:* I'm going to forget you uttered one word. All right? Now you just get the fuck out of here and take your funny stories with you."

Karney didn't move.

"You hear me?" Brendan shouted. Karney caught sight of a telltale fullness at the edge of Brendan's eyes. The anger was camouflage—barely adequate—for a grief he had no mechanism to prevent. In Brendan's present mood neither fear nor argument would convince him of the truth. Karney stood up.

"I'm sorry," he said. "I'll go."

Brendan shook his head, face down. He did not raise it again, but left Karney to make his own way out. There was only Red now; he was the final court of appeal. The story, now told, could be told again, couldn't it? Repetition would be easy. Already turning the words over in his head, he left Brendan to his tears.

Anelisa heard Red come in through the front door; heard him call out a word; heard him call it again. The word was familiar, but it took her several seconds of fevered thought to recognize it as her own name.

"Anelisa!" he called again. "Where are you?"

Nowhere, she thought. I'm the invisible woman. Don't come looking for me. Please God, just leave me alone. She put her hand to her mouth to stop her teeth from chattering. She had to stay absolutely still, absolutely silent. If she stirred so much as a hair's breadth it would hear her and come for her. The only safety lay in tying herself into a tiny ball and sealing her mouth with her palm.

Red began to climb the stairs. Doubtless Anelisa was in the bath, singing to herself. The woman loved water as she loved little else. It was not uncommon for her to spend hours immersed, her breasts breaking the surface like two dream islands. Four steps from the landing he heard a noise in the hallway below—a cough, or something like it. Was she playing some game with him? He turned about and descended, moving more stealthily now. Almost at the bottom of the stairs his gaze fell on a piece of cord which had been dropped on one of the steps. He picked it up and briefly puzzled over the single knot in its length before the noise came again. This

time he did not pretend to himself that it was Anelisa.
He held his breath, waiting for another prompt from
along the hallway. When none came he dug into the side
of his boot and pulled out his switchblade, a weapon he
had carried on his person since the tender age of eleven.
An adolescent's weapon, Anelisa's father had advised
him. But now, advancing along the hallway to the living
room, he thanked the patron saint of blades he had not
taken the old felon's advice.

The room was gloomy. Evening was on the house,
shuttering up the windows. Red stood for a long while
in the doorway anxiously watching the interior for
movement. Then the noise again; not a single sound this
time, but a whole series of them. The source, he now
realized to his relief, was not human. It was a dog most
likely, wounded in a fight. Nor was the sound coming
from the room in front of him, but from the kitchen
beyond. His courage bolstered by the fact that the intruder was merely an animal, he reached for the light
switch and flipped it on.

The helter-skelter of events he initiated in so doing
occurred in a breathless sequence that occupied no more
than a dozen seconds, yet he lived each one in the mi-
nutest detail. In the first second, as the light came on,
he saw something move across the kitchen floor; in the
next, he was walking toward it, knife still in hand. The
third brought the animal—alerted to his planned ag-
gression—out of hiding. It ran to meet him, a blur of
glistening flesh. Its sudden proximity was overpowering: its size, the heat from its steaming body, its vast
mouth expelling a breath like rot. Red took the fourth
and fifth seconds to avoid its first lunge, but on the sixth
it found him. Its raw arms snatched at his body. He

slashed out with his knife and opened a wound in it, but it closed in and took him in a lethal embrace. More through accident than intention, the switchblade plunged into its flesh, and liquid heat splashed up into Red's face. He scarcely noticed. His last three seconds were upon him. The weapon, slick with blood, slid from his grasp and was left embedded in the beast. Unarmed, he attempted to squirm from its clasp, but before he could slide out of harm's way the great unfinished head was pressing toward him—the maw a tunnel—and sucked one solid breath from his lungs. It was the only breath Red possessed. His brain, deprived of oxygen, threw a fireworks display in celebration of his imminent departure: roman candles, star shells, catherine wheels. The pyrotechnics were all too brief; too soon, the darkness.

Upstairs, Anelisa listened to the chaos of sound and tried to piece it together, but she could not. Whatever had happened, however, it had ended in silence. Red did not come looking for her. But then neither did the beast. Perhaps, she thought, they had killed each other. The simplicity of this solution pleased her. She waited in her room until hunger and boredom got the better of trepidation and then went downstairs. Red was lying where the cord's second offspring had dropped him, his eyes wide open to watch the fireworks. The beast itself squatted in the far corner of the room, a ruin of a thing. Seeing it, she backed away from Red's body toward the door. It made no attempt to move toward her, but simply followed her with deep-set eyes, its breathing coarse, its few movements sluggish.

She would go to find her father, she decided, and fled the house, leaving the front door ajar.

It was still ajar half an hour later when Karney arrived. Though he had fully intended to go straight to Red's home after leaving Brendan, his courage had faltered. Instead, he had wandered—without conscious planning—to the bridge over the Archway Road. He had stood there for a long space watching the traffic below and drinking from the half bottle of vodka he had bought on Holloway Road. The purchase had cleared him of cash, but the spirits, on his empty stomach, had been potent and clarified his thinking. They would all die, he had concluded. Maybe the fault was his for stealing the cord in the first place. More probably Pope would have punished them anyway for their crimes against his person. The best they might now hope— *he* might hope—was a smidgen of comprehension. That would almost be enough, his spirit-slurred brain decided: just to die a little less ignorant of mysteries than he'd been born. Red would understand.

Now he stood on the step and called the man's name. There came no answering shout. The vodka in his system made him impudent and, calling for Red again, he stepped into the house. The hallway was in darkness, but a light burned in one of the far rooms and he made his way toward it. The atmosphere in the house was sultry, like the interior of a greenhouse. It became warmer still in the living room, where Red was losing body heat to the air.

Karney stared down at him long enough to register that he was holding the cord in his left hand and that only one knot remained in it. Perhaps Pope had been here and for some reason left the knots behind. However it had come about, their presence in Red's hand offered a chance for life. This time, he swore as he approached the body, he would destroy the cord once and for all. Burn it and scatter the ashes to the four winds. He stooped to remove it from Red's grip. It sensed his nearness and slipped, blood-sleek, out of the dead man's hand and up into Karney's, where it wove itself between his digits, leaving a trail behind it. Sickened, Karney stared at the final knot. The process which had taken him so much painstaking effort to initiate now had its own momentum. With the second knot untied the third was virtually loosening itself. It still required a human agent apparently—why else did it leap so readily into his hand?—but it was already close to solving its own riddle. It was imperative he destroy it quickly, before it succeeded.

Only then did he become aware that he was not alone. Besides the dead, there was a living presence close by. He looked up from the cavorting knot as somebody spoke to him. The words made no sense. They were scarcely words at all, more a sequence of wounded sounds. Karney remembered the breath of the thing on the footpath and the ambiguity of the feelings it had engendered in him. Now the same ambiguity moved him again. With the rising fear came a sense that the voice of the beast spoke *loss*, whatever its language. A rumor of pity moved in him.

"Show yourself," he said, not knowing whether it would understand or not.

A few tremulous heartbeats passed, and then it emerged from the far door. The light in the living room was good, and Karney's eyesight sharp, but the beast's anatomy defied his comprehension. There was something simian in its flayed, palpitating form, but sketchy, as if it had been born prematurely. Its mouth opened to speak another sound. Its eyes, buried beneath the bleeding slab of a brow, were unreadable. It began to shamble out of its hiding place across the room toward him, each drooping step it took tempting his cowardice. When it reached Red's corpse it stopped, raised one of its ragged limbs, and indicated a place in the crook of its neck. Karney saw the knife—Red's, he guessed. Was it attempting to justify the killing, he wondered?

"What are you?" he asked it. The same question.

It shook its heavy head back and forth. A long, low moan issued from its mouth. Then, suddenly, it raised its arm and pointed directly at Karney. In so doing it let light fall fully on its face, and Karney could make out the eyes beneath the louring brow: twin gems trapped in the wounded ball of its skull. Their brilliance, and their lucidity, turned Karney's stomach over. And still it pointed at him.

"What do you want?" he asked it. "Tell me what you want."

It dropped its peeled limb and made to step across the body toward Karney, but it had no chance to make its intentions clear. A shout from the front door froze it in its lolling tracks.

"Anybody in?" the inquirer wanted to know.

Its face registered panic—the too-human eyes rolled in their raw sockets—and it turned away, retreating toward the kitchen. The visitor, whoever he was, called again; his voice was closer. Karney stared down at the corpse, and at his bloody hand, juggling his options, then started across the room and through the door into the kitchen. The beast had already gone. The back door stood wide open. Behind him, Karney heard the visitor utter some half-formed prayer at seeing Red's remains.

wig, which had cost Theodore so much in Vienna, came off. So, after the minimum of persuasion, did her hands.

Dr. Jeudwine came down the stairs of the George house wondering (just wondering) if maybe the grand-pappy of his sacred profession, Freud, had been wrong. The paradoxical facts of human behavior didn't seem to fit into those neat classical compartments he'd allotted them to. Perhaps attempting to be rational about the human mind was a contradiction in terms. He stood in the gloom at the bottom of the stairs, not really wanting to go back into the dining room or the kitchen, but feeling obliged to view the scenes of the crimes one more time. The empty house gave him the creeps. And being alone in it, even with a policeman standing guard on the front step, didn't help his peace of mind. He felt guilty, felt he'd let Charlie down. Clearly he hadn't trawled Charlie's psyche deeply enough to bring up the real catch, the true motive behind the appalling acts that he had committed. To murder his own wife, whom he had professed to love so deeply, in their marital bed; then to cut off his own hand. It was unthinkable. Jeudwine looked at his own hands for a moment, at the tracery of tendons and purple-blue veins at his wrist. The police still favored the intruder theory, but he had no doubt that Charlie had done the deeds—murder, mutilation, and all. The only fact that appalled Jeudwine more was that he hadn't uncovered the slightest propensity for such acts in his patient.

He went into the dining room. Forensic had finished its work around the house; there was a light dusting of fingerprint powder on a number of the surfaces. It was a miracle (wasn't it?) the way each human hand was different; its whorls as unique as a voice pattern or a face. He yawned. He'd been woken by Charlie's call in the middle of the night and he hadn't had any sleep since then. He'd watched as Charlie was bound up and taken away, watched the investigators about their business, watched a cod-white dawn raise its head over toward the river. He'd drunk coffee, moped, thought deeply about giving up his position as psychiatric consultant before this story hit the news, drunk more coffee, thought better of resignation, and now, despairing of Freud or any other guru, was seriously contemplating a bestseller on his relationship with wife-murderer Charles George. That way, even if he lost his job, he'd have found something to salvage from the whole sorry episode. And Freud? Viennese charlatan. What did the old opium eater have to tell anyone?

He slumped in one of the dining-room chairs and listened to the hush that had descended on the house, as though the walls, shocked by what they'd seen, were holding their breaths. Maybe he dozed off a moment. In sleep he heard a snapping sound, dreamed of a dog, and woke up to see a cat in the kitchen, a fat black-and-white cat. Charlie had mentioned this household pet in passing: What was it named? Heartburn? That was it; so named because of the black smudges over its eyes, which gave it a perpetually fretful expression. The cat was looking at the spillage of blood on the kitchen floor, apparently trying to find a way to skirt the pool and reach its food bowl without having to dabble its paws in the mess its master had left behind him. Jeudwine watched it fastidiously pick its way across the kitchen floor and sniff at its empty bowl. It didn't occur to him to feed the thing; he hated animals.

Well, he decided, there was no purpose to be served in staying in the house any longer. He'd performed all the acts of repentance he intended; felt as guilty as he was capable of feeling. One more quick look upstairs, just in case he'd missed a clue, then he'd leave.

He was back at the bottom of the stairs before he heard the cat squeal. Squeal? No: more like *shriek*. Hearing the cry, his spine felt like a column of ice down the middle of his back; as chilled as ice, as fragile. Hurriedly, he retraced his steps through the hall into the dining room. The cat's head was on the carpet, being rolled along by two—by two—(say it, Jeudwine)—*hands*.

He looked beyond the game and into the kitchen, where a dozen more beasts were scurrying over the floor, back and forth. Some were on the top of the cabinet, sniffing around; others climbing the mock-brick wall to reach the knives left on the rack.

"Oh Charlie . . ." he said gently, chiding the absent maniac. "What have you done?"

His eyes began to swell with tears; not for Charlie, but for the generations that would come when he, Jeudwine, was silenced. Simpleminded, trusting generations, who would put their faith in the efficacy of Freud and the holy writ of reason. He felt his knees beginning to tremble, and he sank to the dining room carpet, his eyes too full now to see clearly the rebels that were gathering around him. Sensing something alien sitting on his lap, he looked down, and there were his own two hands. Their index fingers were just touching, tip to manicured tip. Slowly, with horrible intention in their movement, the index fingers raised their nailed heads and looked up at him. Then they turned and began to crawl up his chest, finding fingerholds in each fold of his Italian jacket, in each buttonhole. The ascent ended abruptly at his neck, and so did Jeudwine.

Charlie's left hand was afraid. It needed reassurance, it needed encouragement—in a word, it needed Right. After all, Right had been the Messiah of this new age, the one with a vision of a future without the body. Now the army Left had mounted needed a glimpse of that vision, or it would soon degenerate into a slaughtering rabble. If that happened defeat would swiftly follow. Such was the conventional wisdom of revolutions.

So Left had led them back home, looking for Charlie in the last place it had seen him. A vain hope, of course, to think he would have gone back there, but it was an act of desperation.

Circumstance, however, had not deserted the insurgents. Although Charlie hadn't been there, Dr. Jeudwine had, and Jeudwine's hands not only knew where Charlie had been taken but the route there, and the very bed he was lying in.

Boswell hadn't really known *why* he was running, or to where. His critical faculties were on hold, his sense of geography utterly confused. But some part of him seemed to know where he was going, even if he didn't, because he began to pick up speed once he came to the bridge, and then the jog turned into a run that took no account of his burning lungs or his thudding head. Still innocent of any intention but escape, he now realized that he had skirted the station and was running parallel with the railway line. He was simply going wherever his legs carried him, and that was the beginning and end of it.

The train came suddenly out of the dawn. It didn't whistle, didn't warn. Perhaps the driver noticed him, but probably not. Even if he had, the man could not have been held responsible for subsequent events. No, it was all his own fault, the way his feet suddenly veered toward the track, and his knees buckled so that he fell across the line. Boswell's last coherent thought, as the wheels reached him, was that the train was merely passing from A to B, and, in passing, would neatly cut off his legs between groin and knee. Then he was under the wheels—the carriages hurtling by above him—and the train let out a whistle (so like a scream) which swept him away into the dark.

They brought the black kid into the hospital just after six. The hospital day began early, and deep-sleeping patients were being stirred from their dreams to face another long and tedious day. Cups of gray, defeated tea were being thrust into resentful hands, temperatures were being taken, medication distributed. The boy and his terrible accident caused scarcely a ripple.

Charlie was dreaming again. Not one of his Upper Nile dreams, courtesy of the Hollywood hills, not Imperial Rome or the slave ships of Phoenicia. This was something in black and white. He dreamed he was lying in his coffin. Ellen was there (his subconscious had not caught up with the fact of her death apparently), and his mother and his father. Indeed his whole life was in attendance. Somebody came (was it Jeudwine? The consoling voice seemed familiar) to kindly screw down the lid on his coffin, and he tried to alert the mourners to the fact that he was still alive. When they didn't hear him, panic set in; but no matter how much he shouted, the words made no impression. All he could do was lie there and let them seal him up in that terminal bedroom.

The dream jumped a few grooves. Now he could hear the service moaning on somewhere above his head. *"Man hath but a short time to live. . . ."* He heard the creak of the ropes, and the shadow of the grave seemed to darken the dark. He was being let down into the earth, still trying his best to protest. But the air was getting stuffy in this hole. He was finding it more and more difficult to breathe, much less yell his complaints. He could just manage to haul a stale shiver of air through his aching sinuses, but his mouth seemed stuffed with something, flowers perhaps, and he couldn't move his head to spit them out. Now he could feel the thump of clod on coffin, and Christ alive if he couldn't hear the sound of worms at either side of him, licking their chops. His heart was pumping fit to burst. His face, he was sure, must be blue-black with the effort of trying to find breath.

Then, miraculously, there was somebody in the coffin with him, somebody fighting to pull the constriction out of his mouth, off his face.

"Mr. George!" she was saying, this angel of mercy. He opened his eyes in the darkness. It was the nurse from that hospital he'd been in—she was in the coffin, too. "Mr. George!" She was panicking, this model of calm and patience. She was almost in tears as she fought to drag his hand off his face. *"You're suffocating yourself!"* she shouted in his face.

Other arms were helping with the fight now, and they

were winning. It took three nurses to remove his hand, but they succeeded. Charlie began to breathe again, a glutton for air.

"Are you all right, Mr. George?"

He opened his mouth to reassure the angel, but his voice had momentarily deserted him. He was dimly aware that his hand was still putting up a fight at the end of his arm.

"Where's Jeudwine?" he gasped. "Get him, please."

"The doctor is unavailable at the moment, but he'll be coming to see you later on in the day."

"I want to see him *now*."

"Don't worry, Mr. George," the nurse replied, her bedside manner reestablished, "we'll just give you a mild sedative, and then you can sleep awhile."

"No!"

"Yes, Mr. George!" she replied, firmly. "Don't worry. You're in good hands."

"I don't want to sleep any more. They have control over you when you're asleep, don't you see?"

"You're safe here."

He knew better. He knew he wasn't safe *anywhere*, not now. Not while he still had a hand. It was not under his control any longer, if indeed it had ever been. Perhaps it was just an illusion of servitude it had created these forty-odd years, a performance to lull him into a false sense of autocracy. All this he wanted to say, but none of it would fit into his mouth. Instead he just said: "No more sleep."

But the nurse had procedures. The ward was already too full of patients, and with more coming in every hour (terrible scenes at the YMCA she'd just heard; dozens of casualties, mass suicide attempted), all she could do was sedate the distressed and get on with the business of the day. "Just a mild sedative," she said again, and the next moment she had a needle in her hand, spitting slumber.

"Just listen a moment," he said, trying to initiate a reasoning process with her; but she wasn't available for debate.

"Now don't be such a baby," she chided, as tears started.

"You don't understand," he explained, as she prodded up the vein at the crook of his arm.

"You can tell Dr. Jeudwine everything when he comes to see you." The needle was in his arm, the plunger was plunging.

"No!" he said, and pulled away. The nurse hadn't expected such violence. The patient was up and out of bed before she could complete the plunge, the hypo still dangling from his arm.

"Mr. George," she said sternly. "Will you *please* get back into bed!"

Charlie pointed at her with his stump.

"Don't come near me," he said.

She tried to shame him. "All the other patients are behaving well," she said, "why can't you?" Charlie shook his head. The hypo, having worked its way out of his vein, fell to the floor, still three-quarters full. "I will *not* tell you again."

"Damn right you won't," said Charlie.

He bolted away down the ward, his escape egged on by patients to the right and left of him. "Go, boy, go," somebody yelled. The nurse gave belated chase but at the door an instant accomplice intervened, literally throwing himself in her way. Charlie was out of sight and lost in the corridors before she was up and after him again.

It was an easy place to lose yourself in, he soon realized. The hospital had been built in the late nineteenth century, then added to as funds and donations allowed: a wing in 1911, another after the First World War, more wards in the fifties, and the Chaney Memorial Wing in 1973. The place was a labyrinth. They'd take an age to find him.

The problem was, he didn't feel so good. The stump of his left arm had begun to ache as his painkillers wore off, and he had the distinct impression that it was bleeding under the bandages. In addition, the quarter hypo of sedative had slowed his system down. He felt slightly stupid, and he was certain that his condition must show on his face. But he was not going to allow himself to be coaxed back into that bed, back into sleep, until he'd sat down in a quiet place somewhere and thought the whole thing through.

He found refuge in a tiny room off one of the corridors. Lined with filing cabinets and piles of reports, it smelled slightly damp. He'd found his way into the Memorial Wing, though he didn't know it. The seven-story monolith had been built with a bequest from millionaire Frank Chaney, and the tycoon's own building firm had done the construction job, as the old man's will required. They had used substandard materials and a defunct drainage system, which was why Chaney had died a millionaire, and the wing was crumbling from the basement up. Sliding himself into a clammy niche between two of the cabinets, well out of sight should somebody chance to come in, Charlie crouched on the floor and interrogated his right hand.

"Well?" he demanded in a reasonable tone. "Explain yourself."

It played dumb.

"No use," he said. "I'm on to you."

Still, it just sat there at the end of his arm, innocent as a babe.

"You tried to kill me . . ." he accused it.

Now the hand opened a little, without his instruction, and gave him the once-over.

"You could try it again, couldn't you?"

Ominously, it began to flex its fingers, like a pianist preparing for a particularly difficult solo. *Yes,* it said, *I could; any old time.*

"In fact, there's very little I can do to stop you, is there?" Charlie said. "Sooner or later you'll catch me unawares. Can't have somebody watching over me for the rest of my life. So where does that leave me, I ask myself? As good as dead, wouldn't you say?"

The hand closed down a little, the puffy flesh of its palm crinkling into grooves of pleasure. *Yes,* it was saying, *you're done for, poor fool, and there's not a thing you can do.*

"You killed Ellen."

I did, the hand smiled.

"You severed my other hand, so it could escape. Am I right?"

You are, said the hand.

"I saw it, you know," Charlie said. "I saw it running off. And now you want to do the same thing, am I correct? You want to be up and away."

Correct.

"You're not going to give me any peace, are you, till you've got your freedom?"

Right again.

"So," said Charlie, "I think we understand each other, and I'm willing to do a deal with you."

The hand came closer to his face, crawling up his pajama shirt, conspiratorial.

"I'll release you," he said.

It was on his neck now, its grip not tight, but cozy enough to make him nervous.

"I'll find a way, I promise. A guillotine, a scalpel, I don't know what."

It was rubbing itself on him like a cat now, stroking him. "But you have to do it *my* way, in *my* time. Because if you kill me you'll have no chance of survival, will you? They'll just bury you with me, the way they buried Dad's hands."

The hand stopped stroking and climbed up the side of the filing cabinet.

"Do we have a deal?" said Charlie.

But the hand was ignoring him. It had suddenly lost all interest in bargain making. If it had possessed a nose, it would have been sniffing the air. In the space of the last few moments things had changed—the deal was off.

Charlie got up clumsily, and went to the window. The glass was dirty on the inside and caked with several years of bird droppings on the outside, but he could just see the garden through it. It had been laid out in accordance with the terms of the millionaire's bequest: a formal garden that would stand as as glorious a monument to his good taste as the building was to his pragmatism. But since the building had started to deteriorate, the garden had been left to its own devices. Its few trees were either dead or bowed under the weight of unpruned branches; the borders were rife with weeds; the benches on their backs with their square legs in the air. Only the lawn was kept mowed, a small concession to care. Somebody, a doctor taking a moment out for a quiet smoke, was wandering among the strangled walks. Otherwise the garden was empty.

But Charlie's hand was up at the glass, scrabbling at it, raking at it with his nails, vainly trying to get to the outside world. There was something out there besides chaos, apparently.

"You want to go out," said Charlie.

The hand flattened itself against the window and began to bang its palm rhythmically against the glass, a drummer for an unseen army. He pulled it away from the window, not knowing what to do. If he denied its demands, it could hurt him. If he acquiesced to it and tried to get out into the garden, what might he find? On the other hand, what choice did he have?

"All right," he said, "we're going."

The corridor outside was bustling with panicky activity and there was scarcely a glance in his direction, despite the fact that he was only wearing his regulation pajamas and was barefoot. Bells were ringing, loudspeakers summoning this doctor or that, grieving people being shunted between mortuary and toilet. There was talk of the terrible sights in casualty—boys with no hands, dozens of them. Charlie moved too fast through the throng to catch a coherent sentence. It was best to look intent, he thought, to look as though he had a purpose and a destination. It took him a while to locate the exit into the garden, and he knew his hand was getting impatient. It was flexing and unflexing at his side, urging him on. Then a sign—*To the Chaney Trust Memo-*

rial Garden—and he turned a corner into a backwater corridor, devoid of urgent traffic, with a door at the far end that led to the open air.

It was very still outside. Not a bird in the air or on the grass, not a bee whining among the flowerbeds. Even the doctor had gone, back to his surgeries presumably.

Charlie's hand was in ecstasy now. It was sweating so much it dripped, and all the blood left it so that it had paled to white. It didn't seem to belong to him anymore. It was another being to which he, by some unfortunate quirk of anatomy, was attached. He would be delighted to be rid of it.

The grass was dew-damp underfoot, and here, in the shadow of the seven-story block, it was cold. It was still only six-thirty. Maybe the birds were still asleep, the bees still sluggish in their hives. Maybe there was nothing in this garden to be afraid of; only rot-headed roses and early worms turning somersaults in the dew. Maybe his hand was wrong and there was just morning out here.

As he wandered farther down the garden, he noticed the footprints of the doctor, darker on the silver-green lawn. Just as he arrived at the tree, and the grass turned red, he realized that the prints led one way only.

Boswell, in a willing coma, felt nothing, and was glad of it. His mind dimly recognized the possibility of waking, but the thought was so vague it was easy to reject. Once in a while a sliver of the real world (of pain, of power) would skitter behind his lids, alight for a moment, then flutter away. Boswell wanted none of it. He didn't want consciousness, ever again. He had a feeling about what it would be to wake, about what was waiting for him out there, kicking its heels.

Charlie looked up into the branches. The tree had borne two amazing kinds of fruit.

One was a human being; the surgeon with the cigarette. He was dead, his neck lodged in a cleft where two branches met. He had no hands. His arms ended in round wounds that still drained heavy clots of brilliant color down on to the grass. Above his head the tree swarmed with that other fruit, more unnatural still. The hands were everywhere it seemed, hundreds of them, chattering away like a manual parliament as they debated their tactics. All shades and shapes, scampering up and down the swaying branches.

Seeing them gathered like this the metaphors collapsed. They were what they were: human hands. That was the horror.

Charlie wanted to run, but his right hand was having none of it. These were its disciples, gathered here in such abundance, and they awaited its parables and its prophecies. Charlie looked at the dead doctor and then at the murdering hands, and thought of Ellen, *his* Ellen, killed through no fault of his own, and already cold. They'd pay for that crime—all of them. As long as the rest of his body still did him service, he'd make them pay. It was cowardice, trying to bargain with this cancer at his wrist; he saw that now. It and its like were a pestilence. They had no place living.

The army had seen him, word of his presence passing through the ranks like wildfire. They were surging down the trunk, some dropping like ripened apples from the lower branches, eager to embrace the Messiah. In a few moments they would be swarming over him and all advantage would be lost. It was now or never. He turned away from the tree before his right hand could seize a branch and looked up at the Chaney Memorial Wing, seeking inspiration. The tower loomed over the garden, windows blinded by the sky, doors closed. There was no solace there.

Behind him he heard the whisper of the grass as it was trodden by countless fingers. They were already on his heels, all enthusiasm as they came following their leader.

Of course they would come, he realized, wherever he led, they would come. Perhaps their blind adoration of his remaining hand was an exploitable weakness. He scanned the building a second time and his desperate gaze found the fire escape; it zigzagged up the side of the building to the roof. He made a dash for it, surprising himself with his turn of speed. There was no time to look behind him to see if they were following, he had to trust to their devotion. Within a few paces his furious hand was at his neck, threatening to take out his throat, but he sprinted on, indifferent to its clawing. He reached the bottom of the fire escape and, lithe with adrenaline, took the metal steps two and three at a time. His balance was not so good without a hand to hold the safety railing, but so what if he was bruised? It was only his body.

At the third landing he risked a glance down through the grille of the stairs. A crop of fresh flowers was carpeting the ground at the bottom of the fire escape and was spreading up the stairs toward him. They were coming in their hungry hundreds, all nails and hatred.

Let them come, he thought; let the bastards come. I began this and I can finish it.

At the windows of the Chaney Memorial Wing a host of faces had appeared. Panicking, disbelieving voices drifted up from the lower floors. It was too late now to tell them his life story. They would have to piece that together for themselves. And what a fine jigsaw it would make! Maybe, in their attempts to understand what had happened this morning, they would turn up some plausible solution, an explanation for this uprising that he had not found; but he doubted it.

Fourth story now, and stepping on to the fifth. His right hand was digging into his neck. Maybe he was bleeding. But then perhaps it was rain, warm rain, that splashed onto his chest and down his legs. Two storys to go, then the roof. There was a hum in the metalwork beneath him, the noise of their myriad feet as they clambered up toward him. He had counted on their adoration, and he'd been right to do so. The roof was now just a dozen steps away, and he risked a second look down past his body (it wasn't rain on him) to see the fire escape solid with hands, like aphids clustered on the stalk of a flower. No, that was metaphor again. An end to that.

The wind whipped across the heights, and it was fresh, but Charlie had no time to appreciate its promise. He climbed over the two-foot parapet and onto the gravel-lined roof. Corpses of pigeons lay in puddles, cracks snaked across the concrete, a bucket marked "Soiled Dressings" lay on its side, its contents green. He started across this wilderness as the first of the army fingered their way over the parapet.

The pain in his throat was getting through to his racing brain now, as his treacherous fingers wormed at his windpipe. He had little energy left after the race up the fire escape, and crossing the roof to the opposite side (let it be a straight fall, onto concrete) was difficult. He stumbled once, and again. All the strength had gone from his legs and nonsense filled his head in place of coherent thought. A koan, a Buddhist riddle he'd seen on the cover of a book once, was itching in his memory.

"What is the sound . . . ?" it began, but he couldn't complete the phrase, try as he might.

"What is the sound . . . ?"

Forget the riddles, he ordered himself, pressing his trembling legs to make another step, and then another. He almost fell against the parapet at the opposite side of the roof and stared down. It *was* a straight fall. A parking lot lay below, at the front of the building. It was deserted. He leaned over further and drops of his blood fell from his lacerated neck, diminishing quickly, down, down, to wet the ground. I'm coming, he said to gravity, and to Ellen, and thought how good it would be to die and never worry again if his gums bled when he brushed his teeth, or his waistline swelled, or some beauty passed him on the street whose lips he wanted to kiss, and never would. And suddenly, the army was up on him, swarming up his legs in a fever of victory.

You can come, he said as they obscured his body from head to foot, witless in their enthusiasm, you can come wherever I go.

"What is the sound . . . ?" The phrase was on the tip of his tongue.

Oh yes, now it came to him. *"What is the sound of one hand clapping?"* It was so satisfying, to remember something you were trying so hard to dig up out of your subconscious, like finding some trinket you thought you'd lost forever. The thrill of remembering sweetened his last moments. He pitched himself into empty space, falling over and over until there was a sudden end to dental hygiene and the beauty of young women. They came in a rain after him, breaking on the concrete around his body, wave upon wave of them, throwing themselves to their deaths in pursuit of their Messiah.

To the patients and nurses crammed at the windows it was a scene from a world of wonders—a rain of frogs would have been commonplace beside it. It inspired more awe than terror. It was fabulous. Too soon, it stopped, and after a minute or so a few brave souls ventured out among the litter to see what could be seen. There was a great deal, and yet nothing. It was a rare spectacle, of course—horrible, unforgettable. But there was no significance to be discovered in it; merely the paraphernalia of a minor apocalypse. Nothing to be done but to clear it up, their own hands reluctantly compliant as the corpses were catalogued and boxed for further examination. A few of those involved in the operation found a private moment in which to pray: for explanations, or at least for dreamless sleep. Even the smattering of the agnostics on the staff were surprised to discover how easy it was to put palm to palm.

In his private room in intensive care Boswell came to. He reached for the bell beside his bed and pressed it, but nobody answered. Somebody was in the room with him, hiding behind the screen in the corner. He had heard the shuffling of the intruder's feet.

He pressed the bell again, but there were bells ringing everywhere in the building, and nobody seemed to be answering any of them. Using the cabinet beside him for leverage he hauled himself to the edge of his bed to get a better view of this joker.

"Come out," he murmured through dry lips. But the bastard was biding his time. "Come on . . . I know you're there."

He pulled himself a little farther, and somehow all at once he realized that his center of balance had radically altered, that he had no legs, that he was going to fall out of bed. He flung out his arms to save his head from striking the floor and succeeded in so doing. The breath had been knocked out of him however. Dizzy, he lay where he'd fallen, trying to orient himself. What had happened? Where were his legs, in the name of Jah, *where were his legs?*

His bloodshot eyes scanned the room, and came to rest on the naked feet which were now a yard from his nose. A tag around the ankle marked them for the furnace. He looked up and they were *his* legs, standing there severed between groin and knee, but still alive and kicking. For a moment he thought they intended to do him harm, but no. Having made their presence known to him they left him where he lay, content to be free.

And did his eyes envy their liberty, he wondered, and was his tongue eager to be out of his mouth and away, and was every part of him, in its subtle way, preparing to forsake him? He was an alliance only held together by the most tenuous of truces. Now, with the precedent set, how long before the next uprising? Minutes? Years?

He waited, heart in mouth, for the fall of Empire.

Revelations

THERE had been talk of tornadoes in Amarillo; of cattle, cars, and sometimes entire houses lifted up and dashed to the earth again, of whole communities laid waste in a few devastting moments. Perhaps that was what made Virginia so uneasy tonight. Either that or the accumulated fatigue of traveling so many empty highways with just the deadpan skies of Texas for scenery, and nothing to look forward to at the end of the next leg of the journey but another round of hymns and hellfire. She sat, her spine aching, in the back of the black Pontiac and tried her best to get some sleep. But the hot, still air clung about her thin neck and gave her dreams of suffocation. So she gave up her attempts to rest and contented herself with watching the wheat fields pass and counting the grain elevators bright against the thunderheads that were beginning to gather in the northeast.

In the front of the vehicle Earl sang to himself as he

drove. Beside her, John—no more than two feet away from her but to all intents and purposes a million miles' distance—studied the Epistles of St. Paul, murmuring the words as he read. Then, as they drove through Pantex Village ("They build the warheads here," Earl had said cryptically, then said no more) the rain began. It came down suddenly as evening was beginning to fall, lending darkness to darkness, almost instantly plunging the Amarillo-Pampa Highway into watery night.

Virginia rolled up her window. The rain, though refreshing, was soaking her plain blue dress, the only one John approved of her wearing at meetings. Now there was nothing to look at beyond the glass. She sat, the unease growing in her with every mile they covered to Pampa, listening to the vehemence of the downpour on the roof of the car, and to her husband speaking in whispers at her side.

"Wherefore he saith, Awake thou that sleepest, and rise from the dead, and Christ shall give thee light.

"See then that ye walk circumspectly, not as fools, but as wise,

"Redeeming the time, because the days are evil."

He sat, as ever, upright, the same dog-eared, soft-backed Bible he'd been using for years open in his lap. He surely knew the passages he was reading by heart. He quoted them often enough, and with such a mixture of familiarity and freshness that the words might have been his, not Paul's, newly minted from his own mouth. That passion and vigor would in time make John Gyer America's greatest evangelist, Virginia had no doubt of that. During the grueling, hectic weeks of the tri-state tour her husband had displayed unprecedented confidence and maturity. His message had lost none of its vehemence with this newfound professionalism—it was still that old-fashioned mixture of damnation and redemption that he always propounded—but now he had complete control of his gifts. In town after town—in Oklahoma and New Mexico and now in Texas—the faithful had gathered to listen by the hundreds and thousands, eager to come again into God's kingdom. In Pampa, thirty-five miles from here, they would already be assembling, despite the rain, determined to have a grandstand view when the crusader arrived. They would have brought their children, their savings, and most of all, their hunger for forgiveness.

But forgiveness was for tomorrow. First they had to *get* to Pampa, and the rain was worsening. Earl had given up his singing once the storm began, and was concentrating all his attention on the road ahead. Sometimes he would sigh to himself and stretch in his seat. Virginia tried not to concern herself with the way he was driving, but as the torrent became a deluge her anxiety got the better of her. She leaned forward from the backseat and started to peer through the windshield, watching for vehicles coming in the opposite direction. Accidents were common in conditions like these: bad weather and a tired driver eager to be twenty miles further down the road than he was. At her side John sensed her concern.

"The Lord is with us," he said, not looking up from the tightly printed pages, though it was by now far too dark for him to read.

"It's a bad night, John," she said. "Maybe we shouldn't try to go all the way to Pampa. Earl must be tired."

"I'm fine," Earl put in. "It's not that far."

"You're tired," Virginia repeated. "We all are."

"Well, we could find a motel, I guess," Gyer suggested. "What do you think, Earl?"

Earl shrugged his sizable shoulders. "Whatever you say, boss," he replied, not putting up much of a fight.

Gyer turned to his wife and gently patted the back of her hand. "We'll find a motel," he said. "Earl can call ahead to Pampa and tell them that we'll be with them in the morning. How's that?"

She smiled at him, but he wasn't looking at her.

"I think White Deer's next off the highway," Earl told Virginia. "Maybe they'll have a motel."

In fact, the Cottonwood Motel lay a half mile west of White Deer, in an area of wasteground south of U.S. 60, a small establishment with a dead or dying cottonwood tree in the lot between its two low buildings. There were a number of cars already in the motel parking lot and lights burning in most of the rooms; fellow fugitives from the storm presumably. Earl drove into the lot and parked as close to the manager's office as possible, then made a dash across the rain-lashed ground to find out if the place had any rooms for the night. With the engine stilled, the sound of the rain on the roof of the Pontiac was more oppressive than ever.

"I hope there's space for us," Virginia said, watching the water on the window smear the neon sign. Gyer didn't reply. The rain thundered on overhead. "Talk to me, John," she said to him.

"What for?"

She shook her head. "Never mind." Strands of hair clung to her slightly clammy forehead; though the rain had come, the heat in the air had not lifted. "I hate the rain," she said.

"It won't last all night," Gyer replied, running a hand through his thick gray hair. It was a gesture he used on the platform as punctuation; a pause between one momentous statement and the next. She knew his rhetoric, both physical and verbal, so well. Sometimes she thought she knew everything about him there was to know; that he had nothing left to tell her that she truly wanted to hear. But then the sentiment was probably mutual. They had long ago ceased to have a marriage recognizable as such. Tonight, as every night on this tour, they would lie in separate beds, and he would sleep that deep, easy sleep that came so readily to him, while she surreptitiously swallowed a pill or two to bring some welcome serenity.

"Sleep," he had often said, "is a time to commune with the Lord." He believed in the efficacy of dreams, though he didn't talk of what he saw in them. The time would come when he would unveil the majesty of his visions, she had no doubt of that. But in the meantime he slept alone and kept his counsel, leaving her to whatever secret sorrows she might have. It was easy to be bitter, but she fought the temptation. His destiny was manifest, it was demanded of him by the Lord. If he was fierce with her he was fiercer still with himself, living by a regime that would have destroyed lesser men, and still chastising himself for his pettiest act of weakness.

At last, Earl appeared from the office and crossed back to the car at a run. He had three keys.

"Rooms Seven and Eight," he said breathlessly, the

rain dripping off his brow and nose. "I got the key to the interconnecting door, too."

"Good," said Gyer.

"Last two in the place," he said. "I'll drive the car around. The rooms are in the other building."

The interior of the two rooms was a hymn to banality. They'd stayed in what seemed like a thousand cells like these, identical down to the sickly orange bedcovers and the light-faded print of the Grand Canyon on the pale green walls. John was insensitive to his surroundings and always had been, but to Virginia's eyes these rooms were an apt model for Purgatory. Soulless limbos in which nothing of moment had ever happened, nor ever would. There was nothing to mark these rooms out as different from all the others, but there was something different in *her* tonight.

It wasn't talk of tornadoes that had brought this strangeness on. She watched Earl to-ing and fro-ing with the bags, and felt oddly removed from herself, as though she were watching events through a veil denser than the warm rain falling outside the door. She was almost sleepwalking. When John quietly told her which bed would be hers for tonight, she lay down and tried to control her sense of dislocation by relaxing. It was easier said than done. Somebody had a television on in a nearby room, and the late-night movie was word-for-word clear through the paper-thin walls.

"Are you all right?"

She opened her eyes. Earl, ever solicitous, was looking down at her. He looked as weary as she felt. His face, deeply tanned from standing in the sun at the open-air rallies, looked yellowish rather than its usual healthy brown. He was slightly overweight too, though this bulk married well with his wide, stubborn features.

"Yes, I'm fine, thank you," she said. "A little thirsty."

"I'll see if I can get something for you to drink. They probably have a Coke machine."

She nodded, meeting his eyes. There was a subtext to this exchange which Gyer, who was sitting at the table making notes for tomorrow's speech, could not know. On and off throughout the tour Earl had supplied Virginia with pills. Nothing exotic, just tranquilizers to soothe her increasingly jangled nerves. But they—like stimulants, makeup, and jewelry—were not looked kindly upon by a man of Gyer's principles, and when, by chance, her husband had discovered the drugs, there had been an ugly scene. Earl had taken the brunt of his employer's ire, for which Virginia was deeply grateful. And though he was under strict instructions never to repeat the crime, he was soon supplying her again. Their guilt was an almost pleasurable secret between them. She read complicity in his eyes even now, as he did in hers.

"No Coca-Cola," Gyer said.

"Well, I thought we could make an exception—"

"*Exception?*" Gyer said, his voice taking on a characteristic note of self-regard. Rhetoric was in the air, and Earl cursed his idiot tongue. "The Lord doesn't give us laws to live by so that we can make *exceptions,* Earl. You know better than that."

At that moment Earl didn't much care what the Lord did or said. His concern was for Virginia. She was strong, he knew, despite her Deep South courtesy and the accompanying façade of frailty; strong enough to bring them all through the minor crises of the tour, when the Lord had failed to step in and help his agents in the field. But nobody's strength was limitless, and he sensed that she was close to collapse. She gave so much to her husband; of her love and admiration, of her energies and enthusiasm. More than once in the past few weeks Earl had thought that perhaps she deserved better than the man in the pulpit.

"Maybe you could get me some ice water?" she said, looking up at him with lines of fatigue beneath her gray-blue eyes. She was not, by contemporary standards, beautiful. Her features were too flawlessly aristocratic. Exhaustion though lent them new glamour.

"Ice water, coming right up," Earl said, forcing a jovial tone that he had little strength to sustain. He went to the door.

"Why don't you call the office and have someone bring it over?" Gyer suggested as Earl made to leave. "I want to go through next week's itinerary with you."

"It's no problem," Earl said. "Really. Besides, I should call Pampa, and tell them we're delayed," and he was out of the door and onto the walkway before he could be contradicted.

He needed an excuse to have some time to himself. The atmosphere between Virginia and Gyer was deteriorating by the day, and it was not a pleasant spectacle. He stood for a long moment watching the rain sheet down. The cottonwood tree in the middle of the lot hung its balding head in the fury of the deluge. He knew exactly how it felt.

As he stood on the walkway wondering how he would be able to keep his sanity in the last eight weeks of the tour, two figures walked from the highway and crossed the lot. He didn't see them, though the path they took to Room Seven led them directly across his line of vision. They walked through the drenching rain from the wasteground behind the manager's office—where, back in 1955, they had parked their red Buick—and though the rain fell in a steady torrent it left them both untouched. The woman, whose hairstyle had been in and out of fashion twice since the fifties, and whose clothes had the same period look, slowed for a moment to stare at the man who was watching the cottonwood tree with such rapt attention. He had kind eyes, despite his frown. In her time she might have loved such a man, she thought; but then her time had long gone, hadn't it? Buck, her husband, turned back to her—"Are you coming, Sadie?" he wanted to know—and she followed him onto the concrete walkway (it had been wooden the last time she was here) and through the open door of Room Seven.

A chill ran down Earl's back. Too much staring at the rain, he thought; that and too much fruitless longing. He walked to the end of the patio, steeled himself for the dash across the lot to the office and, counting to three, ran.

Sadie Durning glanced over her shoulder to watch Earl go, then looked back at Buck. The years had not tempered the resentment she felt toward her husband, any more than they'd improved his shifty features or his too-easy laugh. She had not much liked him on June 2, 1955, and she didn't much like him now, precisely thirty years on. Buck Durning had the soul of a philanderer, as her father had always warned her. That in itself was not so terrible; it was perhaps the masculine condition. But it had led to such grubby behavior that eventually she had tired of his endless deceptions. He—unknowing to the last—had taken her low spirits as a cue for a second honeymoon. This phenomenal hypocrisy had finally overridden any lingering thoughts of tolerance or forgiveness she might have entertained, and when, three decades ago tonight, they had checked into the Cottonwood Motel, she had come prepared for more than a night of love. She had let Buck shower, and when he emerged, she had leveled the Smith and Wesson .38 at him and blown a gaping hole in his chest. Then she'd run, throwing the gun away as she went, knowing the police were bound to catch her, and not much caring when they did. They'd taken her to Carson County Jail in Panhandle, and, after a few weeks, to trial. She never once tried to deny the murder. There'd been enough deception in her thirty-eight years of life as it was. And so when they found her defiant, they took her to Huntsville State Prison, chose a bright day the following October, and summarily passed 2,250 volts through her body, stopping her unrepentant heart almost instantaneously. An eye for an eye; a tooth for a tooth. She had been brought up with such simple moral equations. She'd not been unhappy to die by the same mathematics.

But tonight she and Buck had elected to retrace the journey they'd taken thirty years before, to see if they could discover how and why their marriage had ended in murder. It was a chance offered to many dead lovers, though few, apparently, took it up. Perhaps the thought of experiencing again the cataclysm that had ended their lives was too distasteful. Sadie, however, couldn't help but wonder if it had all been predestined, if a tender word from Buck, or a look of genuine affection in his murky eyes, could have stayed her trigger finger and so saved both their lives. This one-night stand would give them an opportunity to test history. Invisible, inaudible, they would follow the same route as they had three decades ago. The next few hours would tell if that route had led inevitably to murder.

Room Seven was occupied, and so was the room beside it. The interconnecting door was wide, and fluorescent lights burned in both. The occupancy was not a problem. Sadie had long become used to the ethereal state; to wandering unseen among the living. In such a condition she had attended her niece's wedding, and later on her father's funeral, standing beside the grave with the dead old man and gossiping about the mourners. Buck however—never an agile individual—was more prone to carelessness. She hoped he would be careful tonight. After all, he wanted to see the experiment through as much as she did.

As they stood on the threshold and cast their eyes around the room in which their fatal farce had been played out, she wondered if the shot had hurt him very much. She must ask him tonight, she thought, should the opportunity arise.

There had been a young woman with a plain but pleasant face in the manager's office when Earl had gone in to book the rooms. She had now disappeared to be replaced by a man of sixty or so, wearing half a week's growth of mottled beard and a sweat-stained shirt. He looked up from a nose-close perusal of yesterday's *Pampa Daily News* when Earl entered.

"Yeah?"

"Is it possible to get some ice water?" Earl inquired.

The man threw a hoarse yell over his shoulder. "Laura May? You in there?"

Through the doorway behind came the din of the late-night movie—shots, screams, the roar of an escaped beast—and then Laura May's response.

"What do you want, Pa?"

"There's a man wants room service," Laura May's father yelled back, not without a trace of irony in his voice. "Will you get out here and serve him?"

No reply came; just more screams. They set Earl's teeth on edge. The manager glanced up at him. One of his eyes was clouded by a cataract.

"You with the evangelist?" he said.

"Yes . . . how did you know it was—?"

"Laura May recognized him. Seen his picture in the paper."

"That so?"

"Don't miss a trick, my baby."

As if on cue Laura May emerged from the room behind the office. When her brown eyes fell on Earl she visibly brightened.

"Oh . . ." she said, a smile quickening her features, "what can I do for you, mister?" The line, coupled with her smile, seemed to signal more than polite interest in Earl; or was that just his wishful thinking? Except for a lady of the night he'd met in Pomca City, Oklahoma, his sex life had been nonexistent in the last three months. Taking a chance, he returned Laura May's smile. Though she was at least thirty-five, her manner was curiously girlish; the look she was giving him almost intimidatingly direct. Meeting her eyes, Earl began to think that his first estimation had not been far off.

"Ice water," he said. "I wondered if you had any? Mrs. Gyer isn't feeling so well."

Laura May nodded. "I'll get some," she said, dallying for a moment in the door before returning into the television room. The din of the movie had abated—a scene of calm, perhaps, before the beast emerged again —and in the hush Earl could hear the rain beating down outside, turning the earth to mud.

"Quite a gully washer tonight, eh?" the manager observed. "This keeps up, you'll be rained out tomorrow."

"People come out in all kinds of weather," Earl said. "John Gyer's a big draw."

The man pulled a face. "Wouldn't rule out a tornado," he said, clearly reveling in the role of doomsayer. "We're just about due for one."

"Really?"

"Year before last, wind took the roof off the school. Just lifted it right off."

Laura May reappeared in the doorway with a tray on which a jug and four glasses were placed. Ice clinked against the jug's sides.

"What's that you say, Pa?" she asked.

"Tornado."

"Isn't hot enough," she announced with casual authority. Her father grunted his disagreement but made no argument in return. Laura May crossed toward Earl with the tray, but when he made a move to take it from her she said, "I'll take it myself. You lead on." He didn't object. It would give them a little while to exchange pleasantries as they walked to the Gyers' room; perhaps the same thought was in her mind. Either that, or she wanted a closer view of the evangelist.

They went together as far as the end of the office

block walkway in silence. There they halted. Before them lay twenty yards of puddle-strewn earth between one building and the next.

"Shall I carry the jug?" Earl volunteered. "You bring the glasses and the tray."

"Sure," she replied. Then, with the same direct look she'd given him before, she said, "What's your name?"

"Earl," he told her. "Earl Rayburn."

"I'm Laura May Cade."

"I'm most pleased to meet you, Laura May."

"You know about this place, do you?" she said. "Papa told you, I suppose."

"You mean the tornadoes?" he asked.

"No," she replied, "I mean murder."

Sadie stood at the bottom of the bed and looked at the woman lying on it. She has very little dress-sense, Sadie thought; the clothes were drab, and her hair wasn't fixed in a flattering way. She murmured something in her semicomatose state, and then—abruptly— she woke. Her eyes opened wide. There was some unshaped alarm in them; and pain too. Sadie looked at her and sighed.

"What's the problem?" Buck wanted to know. He'd put down the cases and was sitting in a chair opposite the fourth occupant of the room, a large man with lean, forceful features and a mane of steel-gray hair that would not have shamed an Old Testament prophet.

"No problem," Sadie replied.

"I don't want to share a room with these two," Buck said.

"Well this is the room where . . . where we stayed," Sadie replied.

"Let's move next door," Buck suggested, nodding through the open door into Room Eight. "We'll have more privacy."

"They can't see us," Sadie said.

"But I can see *them*," Buck replied, "and it gives me the creeps. It's not going to matter if we're in a different room, for Christ's sake." Without waiting for agreement from Sadie, Buck picked up the cases and carried them through into Earl's room. "Are you coming or not?" he asked Sadie. She nodded. It was better to give way to him. If she started to argue now they'd never get past the first hurdle. Conciliation was to be the keynote of this reunion, she reminded herself, and dutifully followed him into Room Eight.

On the bed, Virginia thought about getting up and going into the bathroom where, out of sight, she could take one or two tranquilizers. But John's presence frightened her. Sometimes she felt he could see right into her, that all her private guilt was an open book to him. She was certain that if she got up now and rooted in her bag for the medication, he would ask her what she was doing. If he did that, she'd blurt the truth out for sure. She didn't have the strength to resist the heat of his accusing eyes. No, it would be better to lie here and wait for Earl to come back with the water. Then, when the two men were discussing the tour, she would slip away to take the forbidden pills.

There was an evasive quality to the light in the room. It distressed her, and she wanted to close her lids against its tricks. Only moments before, the light had conjured a mirage at the end of the bed; a moth-wing flicker of substance that had almost congealed in the air before flitting away.

Over by the window, John was again reading under his breath. At first, she caught only a few of the words.

"*And there came out of the smoke locusts upon the earth . . .*" She instantly recognized the passage; its imagery was unmistakable.

"*. . . and unto them was given power, as the scorpions of the earth have power.*"

The verse was from The Revelations of St. John the Divine. She knew the words that followed by heart. He had declaimed them time after time at meetings.

"*And it was commanded them that they should not hurt the grass of the earth, neither any green thing, neither any tree; but only those men which have not the seal of God in their foreheads.*"

Gyer loved Revelations. He read it more often than the Gospels, whose stories he knew by heart but whose words did not ignite him the way the incantatory rhythms of Revelations did. When he preached Revelations, he shared the apocalyptic vision and felt exulted by it. His voice would take on a different note. The poetry, instead of coming out of him, came *through* him. Helpless in its grip, he rose on a spiral of ever more awesome metaphor: from angels to dragons and thence to Babylon, the Mother of Harlots, sitting upon a scarlet-colored beast.

Virginia tried to shut the words out. Usually, to hear her husband speak the poems of Revelations was a joy to her, but not tonight. Tonight the words seemed ripe to the point of corruption, and she sensed—perhaps for the first time—that he didn't really understand what he was saying; that the spirit of the words passed him by while he recited them. She made a small, unintentional noise of complaint. Gyer stopped reading.

"What is it?" he said.

She opened her eyes, embarrassed to have interrupted him.

"Nothing," she said.

"Does my reading disturb you?" he wanted to know. The inquiry was a challenge, and she backed down from it.

"No," she said. "No, of course not."

In the doorway between the two rooms, Sadie watched Virginia's face. The woman was lying of course, the words *did* disturb her. They disturbed Sadie too, but only because they seemed so pitifully melodramatic: a drug—dream of Armageddon, more comical than intimidating.

"Tell him," she advised Virginia. "*Go on*. Tell him you don't like it."

"Who are you talking to?" Buck said. "They can't hear you."

Sadie ignored her husband's remarks. "Go on," she said to Virginia. "Tell the bastard."

But Virginia just lay there while Gyer took up the passage again, its absurdities escalating.

"And the shapes of the locusts were unto horses prepared unto battle; and on their heads were as it were crowns like gold, and their faces were as the faces of men.

"And they had hair as the hair of women, and their teeth were as the teeth of lions."

Sadie shook her head: comic-book terrors, fit to scare children with. Why did people have to die to grow out of that kind of nonsense?

"Tell him," she said again. "Tell him how ridiculous he sounds."

Even as the words left her lips, Virginia sat up on the bed and said: "John?"

Sadie stared at her, willing her on. "Say it. *Say it.*"

"Do you have to talk about death all the time? It's very depressing."

Sadie almost applauded. It wasn't quite the way *she* would have put it, but each to their own.

"What did you say?" Gyer asked her, assuming he'd heard incorrectly. Surely she wasn't challenging him?

Virginia put a trembling hand up to her lips, as if to cancel the words before they came again, but they came nevertheless.

"Those passages you read. I hate them. They're so . . ."

"Stupid," Sadie prompted.

". . . unpleasant," Virginia said.

"Are you coming to bed or not?" Buck wanted to know.

"In a moment," Sadie replied over her shoulder. "I just want to see what happens in here."

"Life isn't a soap opera," Buck chimed in. Sadie was about to beg to differ, but before she had a chance the evangelist had approached Virginia's bed, Bible in hand.

"This is the inspired word of the Lord, Virginia," he said.

"I know, John. But there are other passages . . ."

"I thought you liked the Apocalypse."

"No," she said, "it distresses me."

"You're tired," he replied.

"Oh yes," Sadie interjected, "that's what they always tell you when you get too close to the truth. 'You're tired,' they say, 'why don't you take a little nap?'"

"Why don't you sleep for a while?" Gyer said. "I'll go next door and work."

Virginia met her husband's condescending look for fully five seconds, then nodded.

"Yes," she conceded, "I *am* tired."

"Foolish woman," Sadie told her. "Fight back, or he'll do the same again. Give them an inch and they take half the damn state."

Buck appeared behind Sadie. "I've asked you once," he said, taking her arm, "we're here to make friends. So let's get to it." He pulled her away from the door, rather more roughly than was necessary. She shrugged off his hand.

"There's no need for violence, Buck," she said.

"Ha! That's rich, coming from you," Buck said with a humorless laugh. "You want to see violence?" Sadie turned away from Virginia to look at her husband. *"This* is violence," he said. He had taken off his jacket; now he pulled his unbuttoned shirt open to reveal the shot wound. At such close quarters Sadie's .38 had made a sizable hole in Buck's chest, scorched and bloody. It was as fresh as the moment he died. He put his finger to it as if indicating the Sacred Heart. "You see that, sweetheart mine? *You* made that."

She peered at the hole with no little interest. It certainly was a permanent mark; about the only one she'd ever made on the man, she suspected.

"You cheated from the beginning, didn't you?" she said.

"We're not talking about cheating, we're talking about shooting," Buck returned.

"Seems to me one subject leads to the other," Sadie replied. "And back again."

Buck narrowed his already narrow eyes at her. Dozens of women had found that look irresistible, to judge by the numbers of anonymous mourners at his funeral. "All right," he said, "I had women. So what?"

"So I shot you for it," Sadie replied flatly. That was about all she had to say on the subject. It had made for a short trial.

"Well at least tell me you're sorry," Buck burst out.

Sadie considered the proposition for a few moments and said: "But I'm not!" She realized the response lacked tact, but it was the unavoidable truth. Even as they'd strapped her into the electric chair, with the priest doing his best to console her lawyer, she hadn't regretted the way things had turned out.

"This whole thing is useless," Buck said. "We came here to make peace and you can't even say you're sorry. You're a sick woman, you know that? You always were. You pried into my business, you snooped around behind my back—"

"I did *not* snoop," Sadie replied firmly. "Your dirt came and found me."

"Dirt?"

"Oh yes, Buck, *dirt*. It always was with you. Furtive and sweaty."

He grabbed hold of her. "Take that back!" he demanded.

"You used to frighten me once," she replied coolly. "But then I bought a gun."

He thrust her away from him. "All right," he said, "don't say I didn't try. I wanted to see if we could forgive and forget, I really did. But you're not willing to give an inch, are you?" He fingered his wound as he spoke, his voice softening. "We could have had a good time here tonight, babe," he murmured. "Just you and me. I could have given you a bit of the old jazz, you know what I mean? Time was, you wouldn't have said no."

She sighed softly. What he said was true. Time was she would have taken what little he gave her and counted herself a blessed woman. But times had changed.

"Come on, babe. Loosen up," he said smokily, and began to unbutton his shirt completely, pulling it out of his trousers. His belly was bald as a baby's. "What say we forget what you said and lie down and talk?"

She was about to reply to his suggestion when the door of Room Seven opened and in came the man with the soulful eyes accompanied by a woman whose face rang a bell in Sadie's memory.

"Ice water," Earl said. Sadie watched him move across the room. There'd not been a man as fine as that in Wichita Falls; not that she could remember anyway. He almost made her want to live again.

"Are you going to get undressed?" Buck asked from the room behind her.

"In a minute, Buck. We've got all night, for Christ's sake."

"I'm Laura May Cade," the woman with the familiar face said as she set the ice water down on the table.

Of course, thought Sadie, you're little Laura May. The girl had been five or six when Sadie was last here; an odd, secretive child, full of sly looks. The intervening years had matured her physically, but the strangeness was still in evidence in her slightly off-center features. Sadie turned to Buck, who was sitting on the bed untying his shoes.

"Remember the little girl?" she said. "The one who you gave a quarter to, just to make her go away?"

"What about her?"

"She's here."

"That so?" he replied, clearly uninterested.

Laura May had poured the water and was now taking the glass across to Virginia.

"It's real nice having you folks here," she said. "We don't get much happening here. Just the occasional tornado . . ."

Gyer nodded to Earl, who produced a five-dollar bill and gave it to Laura May. She thanked him, saying it wasn't necessary, then took the bill. She wasn't to be bribed into leaving, however.

"This kind of weather makes people feel real peculiar," she went on.

Earl could predict what subject was hovering behind Laura May's lips. He'd already heard the bones of the story on the way across, and knew Virginia was in no mood to hear such a tale.

"Thank you for the water—" he said, putting a hand on Laura May's arm to usher her through the door. But Gyer cut in.

"My wife's been suffering from heat exhaustion," he said.

"You should be careful, ma'am," Laura May advised Virginia, "people do some mighty weird things—"

"Like what?" Virginia asked.

"I don't think we—" Earl began, but before he could say "want to hear," Laura May casually replied:

"Oh, murder mostly."

Virginia looked up from the glass of ice water in which her focus had been immersed.

"Murder?" she said.

"Hear that?" said Sadie, proudly. "She remembers."

"In this very room," Laura May managed to blurt before Earl forcibly escorted her out.

"Wait," Virginia said as the two figures disappeared through the door. "Earl! I want to hear what happened."

"No you don't," Gyer told her.

"Oh yes she does," said Sadie very quietly, studying the look on Virginia's face. "You'd *really* like to know, wouldn't you, Ginnie?"

For a moment pregnant with possibilities, Virginia looked away from the outside door and stared straight through into Room Eight, her eyes seeming to rest on Sadie. The look was so direct it could almost have been one of recognition. The ice in her glass tinkled. She frowned.

"What's wrong?" Gyer asked her.

Virginia shook her head.

"I asked you what was wrong," Gyer insisted.

Virginia put down her glass on the bedside table. After a moment she said very simply: "There's somebody here, John."

"What do you mean?"

"There's somebody in the room with us. I heard voices before. Raised voices."

"Next door," Gyer said.

"No, from Earl's room."

"It's empty. It must have been next door."

Virginia was not to be silenced with logic. "I heard voices, I tell you. And I saw something at the end of the bed. Something in the air."

"Oh my Jesus," said Sadie, under her breath. "The goddamn woman's psychic."

Buck stood up. He was naked now but for his shorts. He wandered over to the interconnecting door to look at Virginia with new appreciation.

"Are you sure?" he said.

"Hush," Sadie told him, moving out of Virginia's line of vision. "She said she could see us."

"You're not well, Virginia," Gyer was saying in the next room. "It's those pills he fed you . . ."

"No," Virginia replied, her voice rising. "When will you stop talking about the pills? They were just to calm me down, help me sleep."

She certainly wasn't calm now, thought Buck. He liked the way she trembled as she tried to hold back her tears. She looked in need of some of the old jazz, did poor Virginia. Now *that* would help her sleep.

"I tell you I can see things," she was telling her husband.

"That *I* can't?" Gyer replied incredulously. "Is that what you're saying? That you can see visions the rest of us are blind to?"

"I'm not proud of it, damn you," she yelled at him, incensed by this inversion.

"Come away, Buck," Sadie said. "We're upsetting her. She knows we're here."

"So what?" Buck responded. "Her prick of a husband doesn't believe her. Look at him. He thinks she's crazy."

"Well we'll *make* her crazy if we parade around," said Sadie. "At least let's keep our voices down, huh?"

Buck looked around at Sadie and offered up a dirty rag of a smile. "Want to make it worth my while?" he said sleazily. "I'll keep out of the way if you and me can have some fun."

Sadie hesitated a moment before replying. It was probably perverse to reject Buck's advances. The man was an emotional infant and always had been. Sex was one of the few ways he could express himself. "All right, Buck," she said, "just let me freshen up and fix my hair."

An uneasy truce had apparently been declared in Room Seven.

"I'm going to take a shower, Virginia," Gyer said. "I suggest you lie down and stop making a fool of yourself. You go talking like that in front of people and you'll jeopardize the crusade, you hear me?"

Virginia looked at her husband with clearer sight than she'd ever enjoyed before. "Oh yes," she said, without a trace of feeling in her voice, "I hear you."

He seemed satisfied. He slipped off his jacket and went into the bathroom, taking his Bible with him. She heard the door lock, and then exhaled a long, queasy sigh. There would be recriminations aplenty for the exchange they'd just had. He would squeeze every last drop of contrition from her in the days to come. She glanced around at the interconnecting door. There was no longer any sign of those shadows in the air; not the least whisper of lost voices. Perhaps, just *perhaps*, she had imagined it. She opened her bag and rummaged for the bottles of pills hidden there. One eye on the bathroom door, she selected a cocktail of three varieties and downed them with a gulp of ice water. In fact, the ice in the jug had long since melted. The water she drank down was tepid, like the rain that fell relentlessly outside. By morning, perhaps the whole world would have been washed away. If it had, she mused, she wouldn't grieve.

* * *

"I asked you not to mention the killing," Earl told Laura May. "Mrs. Gyer can't take that kind of talk."

"People are getting killed all the time," Laura May replied, unfazed. "Can't go around with her head in a bucket."

Earl said nothing. They had just gotten to the end of the walkway. The return sprint across the lot to the other building was ahead. Laura May turned to face him. She was several inches the shorter of the two. Her eyes, turned up to his, were large and luminous. Angry as he was, he couldn't help but notice how full her mouth was, how her lips glistened.

"I'm sorry," she said, "I didn't mean to get you into trouble."

"Sure I know. I'm just edgy."

"It's the heat," she returned. "Like I said, puts thoughts into people's heads. You know." Her look wavered for a moment; a hint of uncertainty crossed her face. Earl could feel the back of his neck tingle. This was his cue, wasn't it? She'd offered it unequivocally. But the words failed him. Finally, it was she who said: "Do you have to go back there right now?"

He swallowed; his throat was dry. "Don't see why," he said. "I mean, I don't want to get between them when they're having words with each other."

"Bad blood?" she asked.

"I think so. I'm best leaving them to sort it out in peace. They don't want me."

Laura May looked down from Earl's face. "Well I do," she breathed, the words scarcely audible above the thump of the rain.

He put a cautious hand to her face and touched the

down of her cheek. She trembled, ever so slightly. Then he bent his head to kiss her. She let him brush her lips with his.

"Why don't we go to my room?" she said against his mouth. "I don't like it out here."

"What about your Papa?"

"He'll be dead drunk, by now. It's the same routine every night. Just take it quietly. He'll never know."

Earl wasn't very happy with this game plan. It was more than his job was worth to be found in bed with Laura May. He was a married man, even if he hadn't seen Barbara in three months. Laura May sensed his trepidation.

"Don't come if you don't want to," she said.

"It's not that," he replied.

As he looked down at her she licked her lips. It was a completely unconscious motion, he felt sure, but it was enough to decide him. In a sense, though he couldn't know it at the time, all that lay ahead—the farce, the bloodletting, the inevitable tragedy—pivoted on Laura May wetting her lower lip with such casual sensuality. "Ah *shit*," he said, "you're too much, you know that?"

He bent to her and kissed her again, while somewhere over toward Skellytown the clouds gave out a loud roll of thunder, like a circus drummer before some particularly elaborate acrobatics.

In Room Seven Virginia was having bad dreams. The pills had not secured her a safe harbor in sleep. Instead she'd been pitched into a howling tempest. In her dreams she was clinging to a crippled tree—a pitiful anchor in such a maelstrom—while the wind threw cattle and automobiles into the air, sucking half the world up into the pitch black clouds that boiled above her head. Just as she thought she must die here, utterly alone, she saw two figures a few yards from her, appearing and disappearing in the blinding veils of dust the wind was stirring up. She couldn't see their faces, so she called to them.

"Who are you?"

Next door, Sadie heard Virginia talking in her sleep. What was the woman dreaming about? she wondered. She fought the temptation to go next door and whisper in the dreamer's ear, however.

Behind Virginia's eyelids the dream raged on. Though she called to the strangers in the storm they seemed not to hear her. Rather than be left alone, she forsook the comfort of the tree—which was instantly uprooted and whirled away—and battled through the biting dust to where the strangers stood. As she approached, a sudden lull in the wind revealed them to her. One was male, the other female; both were armed. As she called to them to make herself known they attacked each other, opening fatal wounds in neck and torso.

"Murder!" she shouted as the wind spattered her face with the antagonists' blood. "For God's sake, somebody stop them! Murder!"

And suddenly she was awake, her heart beating fit to burst. The dream still flitted behind her eyes. She shook her head to rid herself of the horrid images, then moved groggily to the edge of the bed and stood up. Her head felt so light it might float off like a balloon. She needed some fresh air. Seldom in her life had she felt so strange. It was as though she was losing her slender grip on what was real; as though the solid world were slipping through her fingers. She crossed to the outside door. In the bathroom she could hear John speaking aloud—addressing the mirror, no doubt, to refine every detail of his delivery. She stepped out onto the walkway. There was some refreshment to be had out here, but precious little. In one of the rooms at the end of the block a child was crying. As she listened a sharp voice silenced it. For maybe ten seconds the voice was hushed. Then it began again in a higher key. *Go on,* she told the child, *you cry; there's plenty of reason.* She trusted unhappiness in people. More and more it was *all* she trusted. Sadness was so much more honest than the artificial bonhomie that was all the style these days: that façade of empty-headed optimism that was plastered over the despair that everyone felt in their heart of hearts. The child was expressing that wise panic now, as it cried in the night. She silently applauded its honesty.

In the bathroom, John Gyer tired of the sight of his own face in the mirror and gave some time over to thought. He put down the toilet lid and sat in silence for several minutes. He could smell his own stale sweat. He needed a shower, and then a good night's sleep. Tomorrow: Pampa. Meetings, speeches; thousands of hands to be shaken and blessings to be bestowed. Sometimes he felt so tired, and then he'd get to wondering if the Lord couldn't lighten his burden a little. But that was the Devil talking in his ear, wasn't it? He knew better than to pay that scurrilous voice much attention. If you listened *once,* the doubts would get a hold, the way they had of Virginia. Somewhere along the road, while his back had been turned about the Lord's business, she'd lost her way, and the Old One had found her wandering.

He, John Gyer, would have to bring her back to the path of the righteous; make her see the danger her soul was in. There would be tears and complaints; maybe she would be bruised a little. But bruises healed.

He put down his Bible and went down on his knees in the narrow space between the bath and the towel rack and began to pray. He tried to find some benign words, a gentle prayer to ask for the strength to finish his task, and to bring Virginia back to her senses. But mildness had deserted him. It was the vocabulary of Revelations that came back to his lips, unbidden. He let the words spill out, ven though the fever in him burned brighter with every syllable he spoke.

"What do you think?" Laura May had asked Earl as she escorted him into her bedroom. Earl was too startled by what was in front of him to offer any coherent reply. The bedroom was a mausoleum, founded, it seemed, in the name of Trivia. Laid out on the shelves, hung on the walls and covering much of the floor were items that might have been picked out of any garbage can: empty Coke cans, collections of ticket stubs, coverless and defaced magazines, vandalized toys, shattered mirrors, postcards never sent, letters never read—a limping parade of the forgotten and the forsaken. His eye passed back and forth over the elaborate display and found not one item of worth among the junk and bric-a-brac. Yet all this inconsequentia had been arranged with meticulous care so that no one piece masked another. And— now that he looked more closely—he saw that every item was numbered, as if each had its place in some system of junk. The thought that this was all Laura

May's doing shrank Earl's stomach. The woman was clearly verging on lunacy.

"This is my collection," she told him.

"So I see," he replied.

"I've been collecting since I was six." She crossed the room to the dressing table, where most women Earl had known would have arranged their toiletries. But here were arrayed more of the same inane exhibits. "Everybody leaves something behind, you know," Laura May said to Earl, picking up some piece of dreck with all the care others might bestow on a precious stone and examining it before placing it back in its elected position.

"Is that so?" Earl said.

"Oh yeah. Everyone. Even if it's only a dead match or a tissue with lipstick on it. We used to have a Mexican girl, Ophelia, who cleaned the rooms when I was a child. It started as a game with her, really. She'd always bring me something belonging to the guests who'd left. When she died I took over collecting stuff for myself, always keeping something. As a memento."

Earl began to grasp the absurd poetry of the museum. In Laura May's neat body was all the ambition of a great curator. Not for her mere *art*. She was collecting keepsakes of a more intimate nature, forgotten signs of people who'd passed this way, and who, most likely, she would never see again.

"You've got it all marked," he observed.

"Oh yes," she replied, "it wouldn't be much use if I didn't know who it all belonged to, would it?"

Earl supposed not. "Incredible," he murmured quite genuinely. She smiled at him. He suspected she didn't show her collection to many people. He felt oddly honored to be viewing it.

"I've got some really prize things," she said, opening the middle drawer of the dressing table, "stuff I don't put on display."

"Oh?" he said.

The drawer she'd opened was lined with tissue paper, which rustled as she brought forth a selection of special acquisitions. A soiled tissue found beneath the bed of a Hollywood star who had tragically died six weeks after staying at the motel. A heroin needle carelessly left by X; an empty book of matches, which she had traced to a homosexual bar in Amarillo, discarded by Y. The names she mentioned meant little or nothing to Earl, but he played the game as he felt she wanted it played, mingling exclamations of disbelief with gentle laughter. Her pleasure, fed by his, grew. She took him through all the exhibits in the dressing-table drawer, offering some anecdote or biographical insight with every one.

When she had finished, she said: "I wasn't quite telling you the truth before, when I said it began as a game with Ophelia. That really came later."

"So what started you off?" he asked.

She went down on her haunches and unlocked the bottom drawer of the dressing table with a key on a chain around her neck. There was only one artifact in this drawer. This she lifted out almost reverentially and stood up to show him.

"What's this?"

"You asked me what started the collection," she said. "This is it. I found it, and I never gave it back. You can look if you want."

She extended the prize toward him, and he unfolded

the pressed white cloth the object had been wrapped up in. It was a gun. A Smith and Wesson .38, in pristine condition. It took him only a moment to realize which motel guest this piece of history had once belonged to.

"The gun that Sadie Durning used . . ." he said, picking it up. "Am I right?"

She beamed. "I found it in the scrub behind the motel, before the police got to searching for it. There was such a commotion, you know, nobody looked twice at me. And of course they didn't try and look for it in the light."

"Why was that?"

"The '55 tornado hit, just the day after. Took the motel roof right off; blew the school away. People were killed that year. We had funerals for weeks."

"They didn't question you at all?"

"I was a good liar," she replied, with no small satisfaction.

"And you never owned up to having it? All these years?"

She looked faintly contemptuous of the suggestion. "They might have taken it off me," she said.

"But it's *evidence*."

"They executed her anyway, didn't they?" she replied. "Sadie admitted to it all, right from the beginning. It wouldn't have made any difference if they'd found the murder weapon or not."

Earl turned the gun over in his hand. There was encrusted dirt on it.

"That's blood," Laura May informed him. "It was still wet when I found it. She must have touched Buck's body to make sure he was dead. Only used two bullets. The rest are still in there."

Earl had never much liked weapons since his brother-in-law had blown off three of his toes in an accident. The thought that the .38 was still loaded made him yet more apprehensive. He put it back in its wrapping and folded the cloth over it.

"I've never seen anything like this place," he said as Laura May kneeled to return the gun to the drawer. "You're quite a woman, you know that?"

She looked up at him. Her hand slowly slid up the front of his trousers.

"I'm glad you like what you see," she said.

"Sadie . . . ? Are you coming to bed or not?"

"I just want to finish fixing my hair."

"You're not playing fair. Forget your hair and come over here."

"In a minute."

"Shit!"

"You're in no hurry, are you, Buck? I mean, you're not going anywhere?"

She caught his reflection in the mirror. He gave her a sour glance.

"You think it's funny, don't you?" he said.

"Think *what's* funny?"

"What happened. Me getting shot. You getting the chair. It gives you some perverse satisfaction."

She thought about this for a few moments. It was the first time Buck had shown any real desire to talk seriously. She wanted to answer with the truth.

"Yes," she said, when she was certain that was the answer. "Yes, I suppose it did please me, in an odd sort of way."

"I *knew* it," said Buck.

"Keep your voice down," Sadie snapped, "she'll hear us."

"She's gone outside. I heard her. And don't change the subject." He rolled over and sat on the edge of the bed. The wound did look painful, Sadie thought.

"Did it hurt much?" she asked, turning to him.

"Are you kidding?" he said, displaying the hole for her. "What does it fucking look like?"

"I thought it would be quick. I never wanted you to suffer."

"Is that right?" Buck said.

"Of course. I loved you once, Buck. I really did. You know what the headline was the day after?"

"No," Buck replied, "I was otherwise engaged, remember?"

"'MOTEL BECOMES SLAUGHTERHOUSE OF LOVE,' it said. There were pictures of the room, of the blood on the floor, and you being carried out under a sheet."

"My finest hour," he said bitterly. "And I don't even get my face in the press."

"I'll never forget the phrase. 'Slaughterhouse of Love!' I thought it was romantic. Don't you?" Buck grunted in disgust. Sadie went on anyway. "I got three hundred proposals of marriage while I was waiting for the chair, did I ever tell you that?"

"Oh yeah?" Buck said. "Did they come and visit you? Give you a bit of the old jazz to keep your mind off the big day?"

"No," said Sadie frostily.

"You could have had a time of it. I would have."

"I'm sure you would," she replied.

"Just thinking about it's getting me cooking, Sadie. Why don't you come and get it while it's hot?"

"We came here to talk, Buck."

"We talked, for Christ's sake," he said. "I don't want to talk no more. Now come here. You promised." He rubbed his abdomen and gave her a crooked smile. "Sorry about the blood and all, but I ain't responsible for that."

Sadie stood up.

"Now you're being sensible," he said.

As Sadie Durning crossed to the bed, Virginia came in out of the rain. It had cooled her face somewhat, and the tranquilizers she'd taken were finally beginning to soothe her system. In the bathroom, John was still praying, his voice rising and falling. She crossed to the table and glanced at his notes, but the tightly packed words wouldn't come into focus. She picked up the papers to peer more closely at them. As she did so she heard a groan from the next room. She froze. The groan came again, louder. The papers trembled in her hands. She made to put them back on the table but the voice came a third time, and this time the papers slipped from her hand.

"Give a little, damn you . . ." the voice said. The words, though blurred, were unmistakable; more grunts followed. Virginia moved toward the door between the rooms, the trembling spreading up from her hands to the rest of her body. "Play the game, will you?" the voice came again; there was anger in it. Cautiously, Virginia looked through into Room Eight, holding onto the door lintel for support. There was a shadow on the bed. It writhed distressingly, as if attempting to devour itself. She stood, rooted to the spot, trying to stifle a cry while more sounds rose from the shadow. Not *one* voice this time, but two. The words were jumbled. In her growing panic she could make little sense of them. She couldn't turn her back on the scene, however. She stared on, trying to make some sense of the shifting configuration. Now a smattering of words came clear, and with them, a recognition of the event on the bed. She heard a woman's voice protesting. Now she even began to see the speaker, struggling beneath a partner who was attempting to arrest her flailing arms. Her first instinct about the scene had been correct: it *was* a devouring, of a kind.

Sadie looked up into Buck's face. That bastard grin of his had returned; it made her trigger finger itch. This is what he'd come for tonight. Not for conversation about failed dreams, but to humiliate her the way he had so often in the past, whispering obscenities into her neck while he pinned her to the sheets. The pleasure he took in her discomfort made her seethe.

"Let go of me!" she shouted, louder than she'd intended.

At the door, Virginia said: "Let her alone."

"We've got an audience," Buck Durning grinned, pleased by the appalled look on Virginia's face. Sadie took advantage of his diverted attention. She slipped her arm from his grasp and pushed him off her. He rolled off the narrow bed with a yell. As she stood up, she looked around at the ashen woman in the doorway. How much could Virginia see or hear? Enough to know who they were?

Buck was climbing over the bed toward his sometime murderer. "Come on," he said. "It's only the crazy lady."

"Keep away from me," Sadie warned.

"You can't harm me now, woman. I'm already dead, remember." His exertions had opened the gunshot wound. There was blood smeared all over him; over her too, now she saw. She backed toward the door. There was nothing to be salvaged here. What little chance of reconciliation there had been had degenerated into a bloody farce. The only solution to the whole sorry mess was to get out and leave poor Virginia to make what sense of it she could. The longer she stayed to fight with Buck, the worse the situation would become for all three of them.

"Where are you going?" Buck demanded.

"Out," she responded. "Away from you. I said I loved you, Buck, didn't I? Well . . . maybe I did. But I'm cured now."

"Bitch!"

"Goodbye, Buck. Have a nice eternity."

"*Worthless bitch!*"

She didn't reply to his insults. She simply walked through the door and out into the night.

Virginia watched the shadow pass through the closed door and held on to the tattered remains of her sanity with white-knuckled fists. She had to put these apparitions out of her head as quickly as possible or she knew she'd go crazy. She turned her back on Room Eight. What she needed now was pills. She picked up her handbag, only to drop it again as her shaking fingers rooted for the bottles, depositing the contents of the bag onto the floor. One of the bottles, which she had failed to seal properly, spilled. A rainbow assortment of tablets rolled across the stained carpet in every direction. She bent to pick them up. Tears had started to come, blinding her. She felt for the pills as best she could, feeding half a handful into her mouth and trying to swallow them dry. The tattoo of the rain on the roof sounded louder and louder in her head; a roll of thunder gave weight to the percussion.

And then, John's voice.

"What are you doing, Virginia?"

She looked up, tears in her eyes, a pill-laden hand hovering at her lips. She'd forgotten her husband entirely. The shadows and the rain and the voices had driven all thought of him from her head. She let the pills drop back to the carpet. Her limbs were shaking. She didn't have the strength to stand up.

"I . . . I . . . heard the voices again," she said.

His eyes had come to rest on the spilled contents of bag and bottle. Her crime was spread for him to see quite plainly. It was useless to try and deny anything; it would only enrage him further.

"Woman," he said. "Haven't you learned your lesson?"

She didn't reply. Thunder drowned his next words. He repeated them, more loudly.

"Where did you get the pills, Virginia?"

She shook her head weakly.

"Earl again, I suppose. Who else?"

"No," she murmured.

"Don't lie to me, Virginia!" He had raised his voice to compete with the storm. "You know the Lord hears your lies, as I hear them. And you are *judged*, Virginia! *Judged!*"

"Please leave me be," she pleaded.

"You're poisoning yourself."

"I *need* them, John," she told him. "I really do." She had no energy to hold his bullying at bay; nor did she want him to take the pills from her. But then what was the use of protesting? He would have his way, as always. It would be wiser to give up the booty now and save herself unnecessary anguish.

"Look at yourself," he said, "groveling on the floor."

"Don't start on me, John," she replied. "You win. Take the pills. Go on! *Take them!*"

He was clearly disappointed by her rapid capitulation, like an actor preparing for a favorite scene only to find the curtain rung down prematurely. But he made the most of her invitation, upending her handbag on the bed, and collecting the bottles.

"Is this all?" he demanded.

"Yes," she said.

"I won't be deceived, Virginia."

"That's all!" she shouted back at him. Then more softly: "I swear . . . that's all."

"Earl will be sorry. I promise you that. He's exploited your weakness—"

". . . no!"

"—your weakness and your fear. The man is in Satan's employ, that much is apparent."

"Don't talk nonsense!" she said, surprising herself with her own vehemence. "I *asked* him to supply them." She got to her feet with some difficulty. "He didn't want to defy you, John. It was me all along."

Gyer shook his head. "No, Virginia. You won't save him. Not this time. He's worked to subvert me all along. I see that now. Worked to harm my crusade through you. Well I'm wise to him now. Oh yes. Oh *yes.*"

He suddenly turned and pitched the handful of bottles through the open door and into the rainy darkness outside. Virginia watched them fly and felt her heart sink. There was precious little sanity to be had on a night like this—it was a night for going crazy, wasn't it? with the rain bruising your skull and murder in the air—and now the damn fool had thrown away her last chance of equilibrium. He turned back to her, his perfect teeth bared.

"How many times do you have to be told?"

He was not to be denied his scene after all, it seemed.

"I'm not listening!" she told him, clamping her hands over her ears. Even so she could hear the rain. "I *won't* listen!"

"I'm patient, Virginia," he said. "The Lord will have his judgment in the fullness of time. Now, where's Earl?"

She shook her head. Thunder came again; she wasn't sure if it was inside or out.

"Where is he?" he boomed at her. "Gone for more of the same filth?"

"No!" she yelled back. "I don't know where he's gone."

"You pray, woman," Gyer said. "You get down on your knees and thank the Lord I'm here to keep you from Satan."

Content that his words made a striking exit line, he headed out in search of Earl, leaving Virginia shaking but curiously elated. He would be back, of course. There would be more recriminations, and from her, the obligatory tears. As to Earl, he would have to defend himself as best he could. She slumped down on the bed, and her bleary eyes came to rest on the tablets that were still scattered across the floor. All was not quite lost. There were no more than two dozen, so she would have to be sparing in her use of them, but they were better than nothing at all. Wiping her eyes with the back of her hands, she kneeled down again to gather the pills up. As she did so she realized that someone had their eyes on her. Not the evangelist, back so soon? She looked up. The door out to the rain was still wide open, but he wasn't standing there. Her heart seemed to lose its rhythm for a moment as she remembered the shadows in the room next door. There had been *two*. One had departed; but the other . . . ?

Her eyes slid across to the interconnecting door. It was there, a greasy smudge that had taken on a new solidity since last she'd set eyes on it. Was it that the apparition was gaining coherence, or that she was seeing it in more detail? It was quite clearly human; and just as apparently male. It was staring at her, she had no doubt of that. She could even see its eyes, when she concentrated. Her tenuous grasp of its existence was improving. It was gaining fresh resolution with every trembling breath she took.

She stood up, very slowly. It took a step through the interconnecting door. She moved toward the outside door, and it matched her move with one of its own, sliding with eerie speed between her and the night. Her outstretched arm brushed against its smoky form and, as if illuminated by a lightning flash, an entire portrait of her accoster sprang into view in front of her, only to disappear as she withdrew her hand. She had glimpsed enough to appall her however. The vision was that of a dead man; his chest had been blown open. Was this more of her dream, spilling into the living world? She thought of calling after John, to summon him back, but that meant approaching the door again, and risking contact with the apparition. Instead she took a cautious step backward, reciting a prayer beneath her breath as she did so. Perhaps John had been correct all along. Perhaps she *had* invited this lunacy to herself with the very tablets she was even now treading to powder underfoot. The apparition closed in on her. Was it her imagination, or had it opened its arms, as if to embrace her?

Her heel caught on the skirt of the coverlet. Before she could stop herself she was toppling backward. Her arms flailed, seeking support. Again she made contact with the dream-thing; again the whole horrid picture appeared in front of her. But this time it didn't disappear, because the apparition had snatched at her hand and was grasping it tight. Her fingers felt as though they'd been plunged into ice water. She yelled for it to let her be, flinging up her free arm to push her assailant away, but it simply grasped her other hand too.

Unable to resist, she met its gaze. They were not the Devil's eyes that looked at her—they were slightly stupid, even comical, eyes—and below them a weak mouth which only reinforced her impression of witlessness. Suddenly she was not afraid. This was no demon. It was a delusion, brought on by exhaustion and pills; it could do her no harm. The only danger here was that she hurt herself in her attempts to keep the hallucinations at bay.

Buck sensed that Virginia was losing the will to resist. "That's better," he coaxed her. "You just want a bit of the old jazz, don't you, Ginnie?"

He wasn't certain if she heard him, but no matter. He could readily make his intentions apparent. Dropping one of her hands, he ran his palm across her breasts.

She sighed, a bewildered expression in her beautiful eyes, but she made no effort to resist his attentions.

"You don't exist," she told him plainly. "You're only in my mind, like John said. The pills made you. The pills did it all."

Buck let the woman babble; let her think whatever she pleased, as long as it made her compliant.

"That's right, isn't it?" she said. "You're not real, are you?"

He obliged her with a polite reply. "Certainly," he said, squeezing her. "I'm just a dream, that's all." The answer seemed to satisfy her. "No need to fight me, is there?" he said. "I'll have come and gone before you know it."

The manager's office lay empty. From the room beyond it Gyer heard a television. It stood to reason that Earl must be somewhere in the vicinity. He had left their room with the girl who'd brought the ice water, and they certainly wouldn't be taking a walk together in weather like this. The thunder had moved in closer in the last few minutes. Now it was almost overhead. Gyer enjoyed the noise and the spectacle of the lightning. It fueled his sense of occasion.

"Earl!" he yelled, making his way through the office and into the room with the television. The late movie was nearing its climax, the sound turned up deafeningly loud. A fantastical beast of some kind was treading Tokyo to rubble; citizens fled, screaming. Asleep in a chair in front of this papier-mâché apocalypse was a late middle-aged man. Neither the thunder nor Gyer's calls had stirred him. A tumbler of spirits, nursed in his lap, had slipped from his hand and stained his trousers. The whole scene stank of bourbon and depravity. Gyer made a note of it for future use in the pulpit.

A chill blew in from the office. Gyer turned, expecting a visitor, but there was nobody in the office behind him. He stared into space. All the way across here he'd had a sense of being followed, yet there was nobody on his heels. He canceled his suspicions. Fears like this were for women and old men afraid of the dark. He stepped between the sleeping drunkard and the ruin of Tokyo toward the closed door beyond.

"Earl?" he called out, "answer me!"

Sadie watched Gyer open the door and step into the kitchen. His bombast amazed her. She'd expected his subspecies to be extinct by now. Could such melodrama be credible in this sophisticated age? She'd never much liked church people, but this example was particularly offensive; there was more than a whiff of malice beneath the flatulence. He was riled and unpredictable, and he would not be pleased by the scene that awaited him in Laura May's room. Sadie had already been there. She had watched the lovers for a little while, until their passion became too much for her and had driven her out to cool herself by watching the rain. Now the evangelist's appearance drew her back the way she'd come, fearful that whatever was now in the air, the night's events could not end well. In the kitchen, Gyer was shouting again. He clearly enjoyed the sound of his own voice.

"Earl! You hear me? I'm not to be cheated!"

In Laura May's room Earl was attempting to perform three acts at the same time. One, kiss the woman he had just made love with; two, pull on his damp trousers; and three, invent an adequate excuse to offer Gyer if the evangelist reached the bedroom door before some illusion of innocence had been created. As it was, he had no time to complete any of the tasks. His tongue was still locked in Laura May's tender mouth when the lock on the door was forced.

"Found you!"

Earl broke his kiss and turned toward the messianic voice. Gyer was standing in the doorway, rain-plastered hair a gray skull cap, his face bright with fury. The light thrown up on him from the silk-draped lamp beside the bed made him look massive. The glint in his come-to-the-Lord eyes was verging on the manic. Earl had heard tell of the great man's righteous wrath from Virginia; furniture had been trashed in the past, and bones broken.

"Is there no end to your iniquity?" he demanded to know, the words coming with unnerving calm from between his narrow lips. Earl hoisted his trousers up, fumbling for the zipper.

"This isn't your business . . ." he began, but Gyer's fury powdered the words on his tongue.

Laura May was not so easily cowed. "You get out," she said, pulling a sheet up to cover her generous breasts. Earl glanced around at her; at the smooth shoulders he'd all too recently kissed. He wanted to kiss them again now, but the man in black crossed the room in four quick strides and took hold of him by hair and arm. The movement, in the confined space of Laura May's room, had the effect of an earth tremor. Pieces of her precious collection toppled over on the shelves and dressing table, one exhibit falling against another, and that against its neighbor, until a minor avalanche of trivia hit the floor. Laura May was blind to any damage however. Her thoughts were with the man who had so sweetly shared her bed. She could see the trepidation in Earl's eyes as the evangelist dragged him away, and she shared it.

"Let him be!" she shrieked, forsaking her modesty and getting up from the bed. "He hasn't done anything wrong!"

The evangelist paused to respond, Earl wrestling uselessly to free himself. "What would you know about error, *whore?*" Gyer spat at her. "You're too steeped in sin. You with your nakedness, and your stinking bed."

The bed did stink, but only of good soap and recent love. She had nothing to apologize for, and she wasn't going to let this two-bit Bible-thumper intimidate her.

"I'll call the cops!" she warned. "If you don't leave him alone, I'll call them!"

Gyer didn't grace the threat with a reply. He simply dragged Earl out through the door and into the kitchen. Laura May yelled: "Hold on, Earl. I'll get help!" Her lover didn't answer. He was too busy preventing Gyer from pulling out his hair by the roots.

Sometimes, when the days were long and lonely, Laura May had daydreamed dark men like the evangelist. She had imagined them coming before tornadoes, wreathed in dust. She had pictured herself lifted up by them—only half against her will—and taken away. But the man who had lain in her bed tonight had been utterly unlike her fever-dream lovers; he had been foolish and vulnerable. If he were to die at the hands of a man like Gyer—whose image she had conjured in her desperation—she would never forgive herself.

She heard her father say: "What's going on?" in the far room. Something fell and smashed; a plate perhaps, from off the dresser, or a glass from his lap. She prayed her Papa wouldn't try and tackle the evangelist. He would be chaff in the wind if he did. She went back to the bed to root for her clothes. They were wound up in the sheets, and her frustration mounted with every second she lost searching for them. She tossed the pillows aside. One landed on the dressing table; more of her exquisitely arranged pieces were swept to the floor. As she pulled on her underwear her father appeared at the door. His drink-flushed features turned a deeper red seeing her state.

"What you been doing, Laura May?"

"Never mind, Pa. There's no time to explain."

"But there's men out there—"

"I know. I know. I want you to call the sheriff in Panhandle. Understand?"

"What's going on?"

"Never mind. Just call Alvin and be quick about it or we're going to have another murder on our hands."

The thought of slaughter galvanized Milton Cade. He disappeared, leaving his daughter to finish dressing. Laura May knew that on a night like this Alvin Baker and his deputy could be a long time coming. In the meanwhile God alone knew what the mad-dog preacher would be capable of.

From the doorway, Sadie watched the woman dress. Laura May was a plain creature, at least to Sadie's critical eye, and her fair skin made her look wan and insubstantial despite her full figure. But then, thought Sadie, who am I to complain of lack of substance? Look at me. And for the first time in the thirty years since her death she felt a nostalgia for corporality. In part because she envied Laura May her bliss with Earl, and in part because she itched to have a role in the drama that was rapidly unfolding around her.

In the kitchen an abruptly sobered Milton Cade was blabbering on the phone, trying to rouse some action from the people in Panhandle, while Laura May, who had finished dressing, unlocked the bottom drawer of her dressing table and rummaged for something. Sadie peered over the woman's shoulder to discover what the trophy was, and a thrill of recognition made her scalp tingle as her eyes alighted on her .38. So it was Laura May who had found the gun; the whey-faced six-year-old who had been running up and down the walkway all that evening thirty years ago, playing games with herself and singing songs in the hot still air.

It delighted Sadie to see the murder weapon again. Maybe, she thought, I *have* left some sign of myself to help shape the future. Maybe I *am* more than a headline on a yellowed newspaper, a dimming memory in aging heads. She watched with new and eager eyes as Laura May slipped on some shoes and headed out into the bellowing storm.

Virginia sat slumped against the wall of Room Seven and looked across at the seedy figure leaning on the door lintel across from her. She had let the delusion she had conjured have what way it would with her; and never in her forty-odd years had she heard such depravity promised. But though the shadow had come at her again and again, pressing its cold body onto hers, its icy, slack mouth against her own, it had failed to carry one act of violation through. Three times it had tried. Three times the urgent words whispered in her ear had not been realized. Now it guarded the door, preparing, she guessed, for a further assault. Its face was clear enough for her to read the bafflement and the shame in its features. It viewed her, she thought, with murder on its mind.

Outside, she heard her husband's voice above the din of the thunder, and Earl's voice too, raised in protest. There was a fierce argument going on, that much was apparent. She slid up the wall, trying to make out the words. The delusion watched her balefully.

"You failed," she told it.

It didn't reply.

"You're just a dream of mine, and you failed."

It opened its mouth and waggled its pallid tongue. She didn't understand why it hadn't evaporated. But perhaps it would tag along with her until the pills had worked their way through her system. No matter. She had endured the worst it could offer. Now, given time, it would surely leave her be. Its failed rapes left it bereft of power over her.

She crossed toward the door, no longer afraid. It raised itself from its slouched posture.

"Where are you going?" it demanded.

"Out," she said. "To help Earl."

"No," it told her, "I haven't finished with you."

"You're just a phantom," she retorted. "You can't stop me."

It offered up a grin that was three parts malice to one part charm. "You're wrong, Virginia," Buck said. There was no purpose in deceiving the woman any longer; he'd tired of that particular game. And perhaps he'd failed to get the old jazz going because she'd given herself to him so easily, believing he was some harmless nightmare. "I'm no delusion, woman," he said. *"I'm*

Buck Durning." She frowned at the wavering figure. Was this a new trick her psyche was playing? "Thirty years ago I was shot dead in this very room. Just about where you're standing in fact."

Instinctively, Virginia glanced down at the carpet at her feet, almost expecting the bloodstains to be there still.

"We came back tonight, Sadie and I," the ghost went on. "A one-night stand at the Slaughterhouse of Love. That's what they called this place, did you know that? People used to come here from all over, just to peer in at this very room; just to see where Sadie Durning had shot her husband Buck. Sick people, Virginia, don't you think? More interested in murder than love. Not me . . . I've always liked love, you know? Almost the only thing I've ever had much of a talent for, in fact."

"You lied to me," she said. "You *used* me."

"I haven't finished yet," Buck promised. "In fact I've barely started."

He moved from the door toward her, but she was prepared for him this time. As he touched her, and the smoke was made flesh again, she threw a blow toward him. Buck moved to avoid it, and she dodged past him toward the door. Her untied hair got in her eyes, but she virtually threw herself toward freedom. A cloudy hand snatched at her, but the grasp was too tenuous and slipped.

"I'll be waiting," Buck called after her as she stumbled across the walkway and into the storm. "You hear me, bitch? *I'll be waiting!*"

He wasn't going to humiliate himself with a pursuit. She would have to come back, wouldn't she? And he, invisible to all but the woman, could afford to bide his time. If she told her companions what she'd seen they'd call her crazy; maybe lock her up where he could have her all to himself. No, he had a winner here. She would return soaked to the skin, her dress clinging to her in a dozen fetching ways; panicky perhaps; tearful; too weak to resist his overtures. They'd make music then. Oh yes. Until she begged him to stop.

Sadie followed Laura May out.

"Where are you going?" Milton asked his daughter, but she didn't reply. "Jesus!" he shouted after her, registering what he'd seen. "Where'd you get the goddamn gun?"

The rain was torrential. It beat on the ground, on the last leaves of the cottonwood, on the roof, on the skull. It flattened Laura May's hair in seconds, pasting it to her forehead and neck.

"Earl?" she yelled. "Where are you? *Earl?*" She began to run across the lot, yelling his name as she went. The rain had turned the dust to a deep brown mud; it slopped up against her shins. She crossed to the other building. A number of guests, already woken by Gyer's barrage, watched her from their windows. Several doors were open. One man, standing on the walkway with a beer in his hand, demanded to know what was going on. "People running around like crazies," he said. "All this yelling. We came here for some privacy for Christ's sake." A girl—fully twenty years his junior —emerged from the room behind the beer drinker. "She's got a gun, Dwayne," she said. "See that?"

"Where did they go?" Laura May asked the beer drinker.

"Who?" Dwayne replied.

"The crazies!" Laura May yelled back above another peal of thunder.

"They went around the back of the office," Dwayne said, his eyes on the gun rather than Laura May. "They're not here. Really they're not."

Laura May doubled back toward the office building. The rain and lightning were blinding, and she had difficulty keeping her balance in the swamp underfoot.

"Earl!" she called. "Are you there?"

Sadie kept pace with her. The Cade woman had pluck, no doubt of that, but there was an edge of hysteria in her voice which Sadie didn't like too much. This kind of business (murder) required detachment. The trick was to do it almost casually, as you might flick on the radio, or swat a mosquito. Panic would only cloud the issue; passion the same. Why, when she'd raised that .38 and pointed it at Buck there'd been no anger to spoil her aim, not a trace. In the final analysis, that was why they'd sent her to the chair. Not for doing it, but for doing it too well.

Laura May was not so cool. Her breath had become ragged, and from the way she sobbed Earl's name as she ran it was clear she was close to the breaking point. She rounded the back of the office building, where the motel sign threw a cold light on the wasteground, and this time, when she called for Earl, there *was* an answering cry. She stopped, peering through the veil of rain. It was Earl's voice, as she'd hoped, but he wasn't calling to her.

"Bastard!" he was yelling, "you're out of your mind. Let me alone!"

Now she could make out two figures in the middle distance. Earl, his paunchy torso spattered and streaked with mud, was on his knees in among the soapweed and the scrub. Gyer stood over him, his hands on Earl's head, pressing it down toward the earth.

"Admit your crime, sinner!"

"Damn you, *no!*"

"You came to destroy my crusade. Admit it! Admit it!"

"Go to hell!"

"Confess your complicity, or so help me I'll break every bone in your body!"

Earl fought to be free of Gyer, but the evangelist was easily the stronger of the two men.

"Pray!" he said, pressing Earl's face into the mud. "Pray!"

"Go fuck yourself," Earl shouted back.

Gyer dragged Earl's head up by the hair, his other hand raised to deliver a blow to the upturned face. But before he could strike, Laura May entered the fray, taking three or four steps through the dirt toward them, the .38 held in her quaking hands.

"Get away from him," she demanded.

Sadie calmly noted that the woman's aim was not all it could be. Even in clear weather she was probably no sharpshooter. But here, under stress, in such a downpour, who but the most experienced marksman could guarantee the outcome? Gyer turned and looked at Laura May. He showed not a flicker of apprehension. He's made the same calculation I've just made, Sadie thought. He knows damn well the odds are against him getting harmed.

"The whore!" Gyer announced, turning his eyes heavenward. "Do you see her, Lord? See her shame, her

174

depravity? Mark her! She is one of the court of Babylon!"

Laura May didn't quite comprehend the details, but
the general thrust of Gyer's outburst was perfectly clear.
"I'm no whore!" she yelled back, the .38 almost leaping
in her hand as if eager to be fired. "Don't you *dare* call
me a whore!"

"Please, Laura May . . ." Earl said, wrestling with
Gyer to get a look at the woman, ". . . get out of here.
He's lost his mind."

She ignored the imperative.

"If you don't let go of him . . ." she said, pointing
the gun at the man in black.

"Yes?" Gyer taunted her. "What will you do,
whore?"

"I'll shoot! *I will!* I'll shoot."

Over on the other side of the office building Virginia
spotted one of the pill bottles Gyer had thrown out into
the mud. She stooped to pick it up and then thought
better of the idea. She didn't need pills any more, did
she? She'd spoken to a dead man. Her very touch had
made Buck Durning visible to her. What a skill that
was! Her visions were real, and always had been; more
true than all the secondhand revelations her pitiful husband could spout. What could pills do but befuddle this
newfound talent? Let them lie.

A number of guests had now donned jackets and
emerged from their rooms to see what the commotion
was all about.

"Has there been an accident?" a woman called to
Virginia. As the words left her lips a shot sounded.

"John," Virginia said.

Before the echoes of the shot had died she was making her way toward their source. She already pictured what she would find there: her husband laid flat on the ground; the triumphant assassin taking to his muddied heels. She picked up her pace, a prayer coming as she ran. She prayed not that the scenario she had imagined was wrong, but rather that God would forgive her for willing it to be true.

The scene she found on the other side of the building confounded all her expectations. The evangelist was not dead. He was standing, untouched. It was Earl who lay flat on the miry ground beside him. Close by stood the woman who'd come with the ice water hours earlier. She had a gun in her hand. It still smoked. Even as Virginia's eyes settled on Laura May a figure stepped through the rain and struck the weapon from the woman's hand. It fell to the ground. Virginia followed the descent. Laura May looked startled. She clearly didn't understand how she'd come to drop the gun. Virginia knew, however. She could see the phantom, albeit fleetingly, and she guessed its identity. This was surely Sadie Durning, she whose defiance had christened this establishment the Slaughterhouse of Love.

Laura May's eyes found Earl. She let out a cry of horror and ran toward him.

"Don't be dead, Earl. I beg you, don't be dead!"

Earl looked up from the mud bath he'd taken and shook his head.

"Missed me by a mile," he said.

At his side, Gyer had fallen to his knees, hands clasped together, face up to the driving rain.

"Oh Lord, I thank you for preserving this your instrument, in his hour of need . . ."

Virginia shut out the idiot drivel. This was the man who had convinced her so deeply of her own deluded state that she'd given herself to Buck Durning. Well, *no more*. She'd been terrorized enough. She'd seen Sadie act upon the real world; she'd felt Buck do the same. The time was now ripe to reverse the procedure. She walked steadily across to where the .38 lay in the grass and picked it up.

As she did so, she sensed the presence of Sadie Durning close by. A voice, so soft she barely heard it, said, "Is this wise?" in her ear. Virginia didn't know the answer to that question. What *was* wisdom anyhow? Not the stale rhetoric of dead prophets, certainly. Maybe wisdom was Laura May and Earl, embracing in the mud, careless of the prayers Gyer was spouting, or of the stares of the guests who'd come running out to see who'd died. Or perhaps wisdom was finding the canker in your life and rooting it out once and for all. Gun in hand, she headed back toward Room Seven, aware that the benign presence of Sadie Durning walked at her side.

"Not Buck . . . ?" Sadie whispered, ". . . surely not."

"He attacked me," Virginia said.

"You poor lamb."

"I'm no lamb," Virginia replied. "Not anymore."

Realizing that the woman was perfectly in charge of her destiny, Sadie hung back, fearful that her presence would alert Buck. She watched as Virginia crossed the lot, past the cottonwood tree, and stepped into the room where her tormentor had said he would be waiting. The lights still burned, bright after the blue darkness outside. There was no sign of Durning. Virginia crossed to the interconnecting door. Room Eight was deserted too. Then, the familiar voice.

"You came back," Buck said.

She wheeled around, hiding the gun from him. He had emerged from the bathroom and was standing between her and the door.

"I knew you'd come back," he said to her. "They always do."

"I want you to show yourself—" Virginia said.

"I'm naked as a babe as it is," said Buck, "what do you want me to do: skin myself? Might be fun, at that."

"Show yourself to John, my husband. Make him see his error."

"Oh, poor John. I don't think he wants to see me, do you?"

"He thinks I'm insane."

"Insanity can be very useful," Buck smirked, "they almost saved Sadie from Old Sparky on a plea of insanity. But she was too honest for her own good. She just kept telling them, over and over: 'I wanted him dead. So I shot him.' She never had much sense. But you . . . now, I think *you* know what's best for you."

The shadowy form shifted. Virginia couldn't quite make out what Durning was doing with himself but it was unequivocally obscene.

"Come and get it, Virginia," he said, "grub's up."

She took the .38 from behind her back and leveled it at him.

"Not this time," she said.

"You can't do me any harm with that," he replied. "I'm already dead, remember?"

"*You hurt me*. Why shouldn't I be able to hurt you back?"

Buck shook his ethereal head, letting out a low laugh. As he was so engaged the wail of police sirens rose from down the highway.

"Well, what do you know?" Buck said. "Such a fuss and commotion. We'd better get down to some jazzing, honey, before we get interrupted."

"I warn you, this is Sadie's gun—"

"You wouldn't hurt me," Buck murmured. "I know you women. You say one thing and you mean the opposite."

He stepped toward her, laughing.

"Don't," she warned.

He took another step, and she pulled the trigger. In the instant before she heard the sound, and felt the gun leap in her hand, she saw John appear in the doorway. Had he been there all along, or was he coming out of the rain, prayers done, to read Revelations to his erring wife? She would never know. The bullet sliced through Buck, dividing the smoky body as it went, and sped with perfect accuracy toward the evangelist. He didn't see it coming. It struck him in the throat, and blood came quickly, splashing down his shirt. Buck's form dissolved like so much dust, and he was gone. Suddenly there was nothing in Room Seven but Virginia, her dying husband and the sound of the rain.

John Gyer frowned at Virginia, then reached out for the door frame to support his considerable bulk. He failed to secure it, and fell backward out of the door like a toppled statue, his face washed by the rain. The blood did not stop coming however. It poured out in gleeful spurts; and it was still pumping when Alvin Baker and his deputy arrived outside the room, guns at the ready.

* * *

Now her husband would never know, she thought.
That was the pity of it. He could never now be made to
concede his stupidity and recant his arrogance. Not this
side of the grave, anyhow. He was *safe,* damn him, and
she was left with a smoking gun in her hand and God
alone knew what price to pay.

"Put down the gun and come out of there!" The voice
from the lot sounded harsh and uncompromising.

Virginia didn't answer.

"You hear me, in there? This is Sheriff Baker. The
place is surrounded, so come on out, or you're dead."

Virginia sat on the bed and weighed up the alterna-
tives. They wouldn't execute her for what she'd done,
the way they had Sadie. But she'd be in prison for a
long time, and she was tired of regimes. If she wasn't
mad now, incarceration would push her to the brink and
over. Better to finish here, she thought. She put the
warm .38 under her chin, tilting it to make sure the shot
would take off the top of her skull.

"Is that wise?" Sadie inquired, as Virginia's finger
tightened.

"They'll lock me away," she replied. "I couldn't face
that."

"True," said Sadie. "They'll put you behind bars for
a while. But it won't be for long."

"You must be joking. I just shot my husband in cold
blood."

"You didn't mean to," Sadie said brightly, "you were
aiming at Buck."

"Was I?" Virginia said. "I wonder."

"You can plead insanity, the way I should have done.
Just make up the most outrageous story you can and

stick to it." Virginia shook her head; she'd never been much of a liar. "And when you're set free," Sadie went on, "you'll be notorious. That's worth living for, isn't it?"

Virginia hadn't thought of that. The ghost of a smile illuminated her face. From outside, Sheriff Baker repeated his demand that she throw her weapon through the door and come out with her hands high.

"You've got ten seconds, lady," he said, "and I mean *ten*."

"I can't face the humiliation," Virginia murmured. "I *can't*."

Sadie shrugged. "Pity," she said. "The rain's clearing. There's a moon."

"A moon? Really?"

Baker had started counting.

"You have to make up your mind," Sadie said. "They'll shoot you given half the chance. And gladly."

Baker had reached eight. Virginia stood up.

"*Stop,*" she called through the door.

Baker stopped counting. Virginia threw out the gun. It landed in the mud.

"Good," said Sadie. "I'm so pleased."

"I can't go alone," Virginia replied.

"No need."

A sizable audience had gathered in the lot: Earl and Laura May of course, Milton Cade, Dwayne and his girl, Sheriff Baker and his deputy, an assortment of motel guests. They stood in respectful silence, staring at Virginia Gyer with mingled expressions of bewilderment and awe.

"Put your hands up where I can see them!" Baker said.

Virginia did as she was instructed.

"Look," said Sadie, pointing.

The moon was up, wide and white.

"Why'd you kill him?" Dwayne's girl asked.

"The Devil made me do it," Virginia replied, gazing up at the moon and putting on the craziest smile she could muster.

Down, Satan!

CIRCUMSTANCES had made Gregorius rich beyond all calculation. He owned fleets and palaces; stallions; cities. Indeed he owned so much that to those who were finally charged with enumerating his possessions—when the events of this story reached their monstrous conclusion—it sometimes seemed it might be quicker to list the items Gregorius did *not* own.

Rich he was, but far from happy. He had been raised a Catholic, and in his early years—before his dizzying rise to fortune—he'd found succor in his faith. But he'd neglected it, and it was only at the age of fifty-five, with the world at his feet, that he woke one night and found himself Godless.

It was a bitter blow, but he immediately took steps to make good his loss. He went to Rome and spoke with the Supreme Pontiff; he prayed night and day; he founded seminaries and leper colonies. God, however, declined to show so much as His toenail. Gregorius, it seemed, was forsaken.

Almost despairing, he took it into his head that he could only win his way back into the arms of his Maker if he put his soul into the direst jeopardy. The notion had some merit. Suppose, he thought, I could contrive a meeting with Satan, the Archfiend. Seeing me *in extremis,* would not God be obliged to step in and deliver me back into the fold?

It was a fine plot, but how was he to realize it? The Devil did not just come at a call, even for a tycoon such as Gregorius, and his researches soon proved that all the traditional methods of summoning the Lord of Vermin —the defiling of the Blessed Sacrament, the sacrificing of babes—were no more effective than his good works had been at provoking Yahweh. It was only after a year of deliberation that he finally fell upon his master plan. He would arrange to have built a hell on earth—a modern inferno so monstrous that the Tempter would be tempted, and come to roost there like a cuckoo in a usurped nest.

He searched high and low for an architect and found, languishing in a madhouse outside Florence, a man called Leopardo, whose plans for Mussolini's palaces had a lunatic grandeur that suited Gregorius's project perfectly. Leopardo was taken from his cell—a fetid, wretched old man—and given his dreams again. His genius for the prodigious had not deserted him.

In order to fuel his invention the great libraries of the world were scoured for descriptions of hells both secular and metaphysical. Museum vaults were ransacked for forbidden images of martyrdom. No stone was left unturned if it was suspected something perverse was concealed beneath.

The finished designs owed something to de Sade and to Dante, and something more to Freud and Krafft-Ebing, but there was also much there that no mind had conceived of before, or at least ever dared set to paper.

A site in North Africa was chosen, and work on Gregorius's New Hell began. Everything about the project broke the records. Its foundations were vaster, its walls thicker, its plumbing more elaborate than any edifice hitherto attempted. Gregorius watched its slow construction with an enthusiasm he had not tasted since his first years as an empire builder. Needless to say, he was widely thought to have lost his mind. Friends he had known for years refused to associate with him. Several of his companies collapsed when investors took fright at reports of his insanity. He didn't care. His plan could not fail. The Devil would be bound to come, if only out of curiosity to see this leviathan built in his name, and when he did, Gregorius would be waiting.

The work took four years and the better part of Gregorius's fortune. The finished building was the size of half a dozen cathedrals and boasted every facility the Angel of the Pit could desire. Fires burned behind its walls, so that to walk in many of its corridors was almost unendurable agony. The rooms off those corridors were fitted with every imaginable device of persecution —the needle, the rack, the dark—that the genius of Satan's torturers be given fair employ. There were ovens large enough to cremate families; pools deep enough to drown generations. The New Hell was an atrocity waiting to happen; a celebration of inhumanity that only lacked its first cause.

The builders withdrew, and thankfully. It was rumored among them that Satan had long been watching over the construction of his pleasure dome. Some even claimed to have glimpsed him on the deeper levels, where the chill was so profound it froze the piss in your bladder. There was some evidence to support the belief in supernatural presences converging on the building as it neared completion, not least the cruel death of Leopardo, who had either thrown himself or—the superstitious argued—been pitched *through* his sixth-story hotel window. He was buried with due extravagance.

So now, alone in hell, Gregorius waited.

He did not have to wait long. He had been there a day, no more, when he heard noises from the lower depths. Anticipation brimming, he went in search of their source, but found only the roiling of excrement baths and the rattling of ovens. He returned to his suite of chambers on the ninth level and waited. The noises came again; again he went in search of their source; again he came away disappointed.

The disturbances did not abate, however. In the days that followed scarcely ten minutes would pass without his hearing some sound of occupancy. The Prince of Darkness was here, Gregorius could have no doubt of it, but he was keeping to the shadows. Gregorius was content to play along. It was the Devil's party, after all. His to play whatever game he chose.

But during the long and often lonely months that followed, Gregorius wearied of this hide-and-seek and began to demand that Satan show himself. His voice rang unanswered down the deserted corridors, however, until his throat was bruised with shouting. Thereafter he went about his searches stealthily, hoping to catch his tenant unawares. But the Apostate Angel always flitted away before Gregorius could step within sight of him.

They would play a waiting game, it seemed, he and Satan, chasing each other's tails through ice and fire and ice again. Gregorius told himself to be patient. The Devil had come, hadn't he? Wasn't that his fingerprint on the door handle? His turd on the stairs? Sooner or later the Fiend would show his face, and Gregorius would spit on it.

The world outside went on its way, and Gregorius was consigned to the company of other recluses who had been ruined by wealth. His Folly, as it was known, was not entirely without visitors, however. There were a few who had loved him too much to forget him—a few, also, who had profited by him and hoped to turn his madness to their further profit—who dared the gates of the New Hell. These visitors made the journey without announcing their intentions, fearing the disapproval of their friends. The investigations into their subsequent disappearance never reached as far as North Africa.

And in his folly Gregorius still chased the Serpent, and the Serpent still eluded him, leaving only more and more terrible signs of his occupancy as the months went by.

It was the wife of one of the missing visitors who finally discovered the truth and alerted the authorities. Gregorius's Folly was put under surveillance, and finally—some three years after its completion—a quartet of officers braved the threshold.

Without maintenance the Folly had begun to deteriorate badly. The lights had failed on many of the levels, its walls had cooled, its pitch pits solidified. But as the officers advanced through the gloomy vaults in search of Gregorius they came upon ample evidence that despite its decrepit condition the New Hell was in good working order. There were bodies in the ovens, their faces wide and black. There were human remains seated and strung up in many of the rooms, gouged and pricked and slit to death.

Their terror grew with every door they pressed open, every new abomination their fevered eyes fell upon.

Two of the four who crossed the threshold never reached the chamber at its center. Terror overtook them on their way and they fled, only to be waylaid in some choked passageway and added to the hundreds who had perished in the Folly since Satan had taken residence.

Of the pair who finally unearthed the perpetrator, only one had courage enough to tell his story, though the scenes he faced there in the Folly's heart were almost too terrible to bear relating.

There was no sign of Satan, of course. There was only Gregorius. The master builder, finding no one to inhabit the house he had sweated over, had occupied it himself. He had with him a few disciples whom he'd mustered over the years. They, like him, seemed unremarkable creatures. But there was not a torture device in the building they had not made thorough and merciless use of.

Gregorius did not resist his arrest. Indeed he seemed pleased to have a platform from which to boast of his butcheries. Then, and later at his trial, he spoke freely of his ambition and his appetite; and of how much *more* blood he would spill if they would only set him free to do so. Enough to drown all belief and its delusions, he swore. And still he would not be satisfied. For God was rotting in paradise, and Satan in the abyss, and who was to stop him?

He was much reviled during the trial, and later in the asylum where, under some suspicious circumstances, he died barely two months later. The Vatican expunged all report of him from its records. The seminaries founded in his unholy name were dissolved.

But there were those, even among the cardinals, who could not put his unrepentant malice out of their heads, and—in the privacy of their doubt—wondered if he had not succeeded in his strategy. If, in giving up all hope of angels—fallen or otherwise—he had not become one himself.

Or all that earth could bear of such phenomena.

The
Age of
Desire

THE burning man propelled himself down the steps of the Hume Laboratories as the police car—summoned, he presumed, by the alarm either Welles or Dance had set off upstairs—appeared at the gate and swung up the driveway. As he ran from the door the car screeched up to the steps and discharged its human cargo. He waited in the shadows, too exhausted by terror to run any farther, certain that they would see him. But they disappeared through the swing doors without so much as a glance toward his torment. Am I on fire at all? he wondered. Was this horrifying spectacle—his flesh baptized with a polished flame that seared but failed to consume—simply a hallucination, for his eyes and his eyes only? If so, perhaps all that he had suffered up in the laboratory had also been delirium. Perhaps he had not truly committed the crimes he had fled from, the heat in his flesh licking him into ecstasies.

He looked down his body. His exposed skin still

crawled with livid dots of fire, but one by one they were being extinguished. He was going out, he realized, like a neglected bonfire. The sensations that had suffused him—so intense and so demanding that they had been as like pain as pleasure—were finally deserting his nerve endings, leaving a numbness for which he was grateful. His body, now appearing from beneath the veil of fire, was in a sorry condition. His skin was a panic-map of scratches, his clothes torn to shreds, his hands sticky with coagulating blood; blood, he knew, that was not his own. There was no avoiding the bitter truth. He *had* done all he had imagined doing. Even now the officers would be staring down at his atrocious handi-work.

He crept away from his niche beside the door and down the driveway, keeping a lookout for the return of the two policemen. Neither reappeared. The street beyond the gate was deserted. He started to run. He had managed only a few paces when the alarm in the building behind him was abruptly cut off. For several seconds his ears rang in sympathy with the silenced bell. Then, eerily, he began to hear the sound of heat—the surreptitious murmuring of embers—distant enough that he didn't panic, yet close as his heartbeat.

He limped on to put as much distance as he could between him and his felonies before they were discovered. But however fast he ran, the heat went with him, safe in some backwater of his gut, threatening with every desperate step he took to ignite him afresh.

It took Dooley several seconds to identify the cacophony he was hearing from the upper floor now that McBride had hushed the alarm bell. It was the high-pitched chattering of monkeys, and it came from one of the many rooms down the corridor to his right.

"Virgil," he called down the stairwell. "Get up here."

Not waiting for his partner to join him, Dooley headed off toward the source of the din. Halfway along the corridor the smell of static and new carpeting gave way to a more pungent combination: urine, disinfectant and rotting fruit. Dooley slowed his advance. He didn't like the smell any more than he liked the hysteria in the babble of monkey voices. But McBride was slow in answering his call, and after a short hesitation, Dooley's curiosity got the better of his disquiet. Hand on truncheon, he approached the open door and stepped in. His appearance sparked off another wave of frenzy from the animals, a dozen or so rhesus monkeys. They threw themselves around in their cages, somersaulting, screeching and berating the wire mesh. Their excitement was infectious. Dooley could feel the sweat begin to squeeze from his pores.

"Is there anybody here?" he called out.

The only reply came from the prisoners: more hysteria, more cage rattling. He stared across the room at them. They stared back, their teeth bared in fear or welcome; Dooley didn't know which, nor did he wish to test their intentions. He kept well clear of the bench on which the cages were lined up as he began a perfunctory search of the laboratory.

"I wondered what the hell the smell was," McBride said, appearing at the door.

"Just animals," Dooley replied.

"Don't they ever wash? Filthy buggers."

"Anything downstairs?"

"Nope," McBride said, crossing to the cages. The monkeys met his advance with more gymnastics. "Just the alarm."

"Nothing up here either," Dooley said. He was about to add, *"Don't do that,"* to prevent his partner putting his finger to the mesh, but before the words were out one of the animals seized the proffered digit and bit it. McBride wrested his finger free and threw a blow back against the mesh in retaliation. Squealing its anger, the occupant flung its scrawny body about in a lunatic fandango that threatened to pitch cage and monkey alike onto the floor.

"You'll need a tetanus shot for that," Dooley commented.

"Shit!" said McBride, "what's wrong with the little bastard anyhow?"

"Maybe they don't like strangers."

"They're out of their tiny minds." McBride sucked ruminatively on his finger, then spat. "I mean, look at them."

Dooley didn't answer.

"I said, *look* . . ." McBride repeated.

Very quietly, Dooley said: "Over here."

"What is it?"

"Just come over here."

McBride drew his gaze from the row of cages and across the cluttered work surfaces to where Dooley was staring at the ground, the look on his face one of fascinated revulsion. McBride neglected his finger sucking and threaded his way among the benches and stools to where his partner stood.

"Under there," Dooley murmured.

On the scuffed floor at Dooley's feet was a woman's

beige shoe; beneath the bench was the shoe's owner. To judge by her cramped position she had either been secreted there by the miscreant or dragged herself out of sight and died in hiding.

"Is she dead?" McBride asked.

"Look at her, for Christ's sake," Dooley replied, "she's been torn open."

"We've got to check for vital signs," McBride reminded him. Dooley made no move to comply, so McBride squatted down in front of the victim and checked for a pulse at her ravaged neck. There was none. Her skin was still warm beneath his fingers however. A gloss of saliva on her cheek had not yet dried.

Dooley, calling in his report, looked down at the deceased. The worst of her wounds, on the upper torso, were masked by McBride's crouching body. All he could see was a fall of auburn hair and her legs, one foot shoeless, protruding from her hiding place. They were beautiful legs, he thought. He might have whistled after such legs once upon a time.

"She's a doctor or a technician," McBride said. "She's wearing a lab coat." Or she had been. In fact the coat had been ripped open, as had the layers of clothing beneath, and then, as if to complete the exhibition, the skin and muscle beneath that. McBride peered into her chest. The sternum had been snapped and the heart teased from its seat, as if her killer had wanted to take it as a keepsake and been interrupted in the act. He perused her without squeamishness; he had always prided himself on his strong stomach.

"Are you satisfied she's dead?"

"Never saw deader."

"Carnegie's coming down," Dooley said, crossing to

one of the sinks. Careless of fingerprints, he turned on the tap and splashed a handful of cold water onto his face. When he looked up from his ablutions McBride had left off his tête-à-tête with the corpse and was walking down the laboratory toward a bank of machinery.

"What do they do here, for Christ's sake?" he remarked. "Look at all this stuff."

"Some kind of research facility," Dooley said.

"What do they research?"

"How the hell do I know?" Dooley snapped. The ceaseless chatterings of the monkeys and the proximity of the dead woman made him want to desert the place. "Let's leave it be, huh?"

McBride ignored Dooley's request; equipment fascinated him. He stared entranced at the encephalograph and electrocardiograph; at the printout units still disgorging yards of blank paper onto the floor; at the video display monitors and the consoles. The scene brought the *Marie Celeste* to his mind. This was like some deserted ship of science—still humming some tuneless song to itself as it sailed on, though there was neither captain nor crew left behind to attend upon it.

Beyond the wall of equipment was a window, no more than a yard square. McBride had assumed it let on to the exterior of the building, but now that he looked more closely he realized it did not. A test chamber lay beyond the banked units.

"Dooley . . . ?" he said, glancing around. The man had gone, however, down to meet Carnegie presumably. Content to be left to his exploration, McBride returned his attention to the window. There was no light on inside. Curious, he walked around the back of the banked equipment until he found the chamber door. It was ajar. Without hesitation, he stepped through.

Most of the light through the window was blocked by the instruments on the other side; the interior was dark. It took McBride's eyes a few seconds to get a true impression of the chaos the chamber contained: the overturned table; the chair of which somebody had made matchwood; the tangle of cables and demolished equipment—cameras, perhaps, to monitor proceedings in the chamber?—clusters of lights which had been similarly smashed. No professional vandal could have made a more thorough job of breaking up the chamber than had been made.

There was a smell in the air which McBride recognized but, irritatingly, couldn't place. He stood still, tantalized by the scent. The sound of sirens rose from down the corridor outside; Carnegie would be here in moments. Suddenly, the smell's association came to him. It was the same scent that twitched in his nostrils when, after making love to Jessica and—as was his ritual—washing himself, he returned from the bathroom to bedroom. It was the smell of sex. He smiled.

His face was still registering pleasure when a heavy object sliced through the air and met his nose. He felt the cartilage give and a rush of blood come. He took two or three giddy steps backward, thereby avoiding the subsequent slice, but lost his footing in the disarray. He fell awkwardly in a litter of glass shards and looked up to see his assailant, wielding a metal bar, moving toward him. The man's face resembled one of the monkeys; the same yellowed teeth, the same rabid eyes. *"No!"* the man shouted, as he brought his makeshift club down on McBride, who managed to ward off the blow with his arm, snatching at the weapon in so doing. The attack had taken him unawares but now, with the pain in his mashed nose to add fury to his response, he was more than the equal of the aggressor. He plucked the club from the man, sweets from a babe, and leaped, roaring, to his feet. Any precepts he might once have been taught about arrest techniques had fled from his mind. He lay a hail of blows on the man's head and shoulders, forcing him backward across the chamber. The man cowered beneath the assault and eventually slumped, whimpering, against the wall. Only now, with his antagonist abused to the verge of unconsciousness, did McBride's furor falter. He stood in the middle of the chamber, gasping for breath, and watched the beaten man slip down the wall. He had made a profound error. The assailant, he now realized, was dressed in a white laboratory coat. He was, as Dooley was irritatingly fond of saying, on the side of the angels.

"Damn," said McBride, "shit, hell and damn."

The man's eyes flickered open, and he gazed up at McBride. His grasp on consciousness was evidently tenuous, but a look of recognition crossed his wide-browed, somber face. Or rather, recognition's absence.

"You're not him," he murmured.

"Who?" said McBride, realizing he might yet salvage his reputation from this fiasco if he could squeeze a clue from the witness. "Who did you think I was?"

The man opened his mouth, but no words emerged. Eager to hear the testimony, McBride crouched beside him and said: "Who did you think you were attacking?"

Again the mouth opened; again no audible words

emerged. McBride pressed his suit. "It's important," he said, "just tell me who was here."

The man strove to voice his reply. McBride pressed his ear to the trembling mouth.

"In a pig's eye," the man said, then passed out, leaving McBride to curse his father, who'd bequeathed him a temper he was afraid he would probably live to regret. But then, what was living for?

Inspector Carnegie was used to boredom. For every rare moment of genuine discovery his professional life had furnished him with, he had endured hour upon hour of waiting for bodies to be photographed and examined, for lawyers to be bargained with and suspects intimidated. He had long ago given up attempting to fight this tide of ennui and, after his fashion, had learned the art of going with the flow. The processes of investigation could not be hurried. The wise man, he had come to appreciate, let the pathologists, the lawyers and all their tribes have their tardy way. All that mattered, in the fullness of time, was that the finger be pointed and that the guilty quake.

Now, with the clock on the laboratory wall reading twelve fifty-three a.m., and even the monkeys hushed in their cages, he sat at one of the benches and waited for Hendrix to finish his calculations. The surgeon consulted the thermometer, then stripped off his gloves like a second skin and threw them down onto the sheet on which the deceased lay. "It's always difficult," the doctor said, "fixing time of death. She's lost less than three degrees. I'd say she's been dead under two hours."

"The officers arrived at a quarter to twelve," Carnegie said, "so she died maybe half an hour before that?"

"Something of that order."

"Was she put in there?" he asked, indicating the place beneath the bench.

"Oh certainly. There's no way she hid herself away. Not with those injuries. They're quite something, aren't they?"

Carnegie stared at Hendrix. The man had presumably seen hundreds of corpses, in every conceivable condition, but the enthusiasm in his pinched features was unqualified. Carnegie found that mystery more fascinating in its way than that of the dead woman and her slaughterer. How could anyone possibly enjoy taking the rectal temperature of a corpse? It confounded him. But the pleasure was there, gleaming in the man's eyes.

"Motive?" Carnegie asked.

"Pretty explicit, isn't it? Rape. There's been very thorough molestation; contusions around the vagina; copious semen deposits. Plenty to work with."

"And the wounds on her torso?"

"Ragged. Tears more than cuts."

"Weapon?"

"Don't know." Hendrix made an inverted U of his mouth. "I mean, the flesh has been *mauled*. If it weren't for the rape evidence I'd be tempted to suggest an animal."

"Dog, you mean?"

"I was thinking more of a tiger," Hendrix said.

Carnegie frowned. "Tiger?"

"Joke," Hendrix replied, "I was making a joke, Carnegie. My Christ, do you have *any* sense of irony?"

"This isn't funny," Carnegie said.

"I'm not laughing," Hendrix replied with a sour look.

"The man McBride found in the test chamber?"

"What about him?"

"Suspect?"

"Not in a thousand years. We're looking for a *maniac*, Carnegie. Big, strong. Wild."

"And the wounding? Before or after?"

Hendrix scowled. "I don't know. Postmortem will give us more. But for what it's worth, I think our man was in a frenzy. I'd say the wounding and the rape were probably simultaneous."

Carnegie's normally phlegmatic features registered something close to shock. "Simultaneous?"

Hendrix shrugged. "Lust's a funny thing," he said.

"Hilarious," came the appalled reply.

As was his wont, Carnegie had his driver deposit him half a mile from his doorstep to allow him a head-clearing walk before home, hot chocolate and slumber. The ritual was observed religiously, even when the Inspector was dog-tired. He used to stroll to wind down before stepping over the threshold. Long experience had taught him that taking his professional concerns into the house assisted neither the investigation nor his domestic life. He had learned the lesson too late to keep his wife from leaving him and his children from estrangement, but he applied the principle still.

Tonight, he walked slowly to allow the distressing scenes the evening had brought to recede somewhat. The route took him past a small cinema which, he had read in the local press, was soon to be demolished. He was not surprised. Though he was no cineaste the fare the flea pit provided had degenerated in recent years. The week's offering was a case in point: a double bill of horror movies. Lurid and derivative stuff to judge by the posters, with their crude graphics and their unashamed hyperbole. *"You May Never Sleep Again!"* one of the hook lines read; and beneath it a woman—very much awake—cowered in the shadow of a two-headed man. What trivial images the populists conjured to stir some fear in their audiences. The walking dead; nature grown vast and rampant in a miniature world; blood drinkers, omens, fire walkers, thunderstorms and all the other foolishness the public cowered before. It was all so laughably trite. Among that catalogue of penny dreadfuls there wasn't one that equaled the banality of human appetite, which horror (or the consequences of same) he saw every week of his working life. Thinking of it, his mind thumbed through a dozen snapshots: the dead by torchlight, face down and thrashed to oblivion; and the living too, meeting his mind's eye with hunger in theirs —for sex, for narcotics, for others' pain. Why didn't they put *that* on the posters?

As he reached his home a child squealed in the shadows beside his garage; the cry stopped him in his tracks. It came again, and this time he recognized it for what it was. No child at all but a cat, or cats, exchanging love calls in the darkened passageway. He went to the place to shoo them off. Their venereal secretions made the passage stink. He didn't need to yell; his footfall was sufficient to scare them away. They darted in all directions, not two, but half a dozen of them. A veritable orgy had been underway apparently. He had arrived on the spot too late however. The stench of their seductions was overpowering.

* * *

Carnegie looked blankly at the elaborate setup of monitors and video recorders that dominated his office.

"What in Christ's name is this about?" he wanted to know.

"The video tapes," said Boyle, his number two, "from the laboratory. I think you ought to have a look at them, sir."

Though they had worked in tandem for seven months, Boyle was not one of Carnegie's favorite officers; you could practically smell the ambition off his smooth hide. In someone half his age again such greed would have been objectionable. In a man of thirty it verged on the obscene. This present display—the mustering of equipment ready to confront Carnegie when he walked in at eight in the morning—was just Boyle's style: flashy and redundant.

"Why so many screens?" Carnegie asked acidly. "Do I get it in stereo, too?"

"They had three cameras running simultaneously, sir. Covering the experiment from several angles."

"What experiment?"

Boyle gestured for his superior to sit down. Obsequious to a fault, aren't you? thought Carnegie; much good it'll do you.

"Right," Boyle instructed the technician at the recorders, "roll the tapes."

Carnegie sipped at the cup of hot chocolate he had brought in with him. The beverage was a weakness of his, verging on addiction. On the days when the machine supplying it broke down he was an unhappy man indeed. He looked at the three screens. Suddenly, a title.

"Project Blind Boy," the words read. *"Restricted."*

"Blind Boy?" said Carnegie. "What, or *who*, is that?"

"It's obviously a code word of some kind," Boyle said.

"Blind Boy. Blind Boy." Carnegie repeated the phrase as if to beat it into submission, but before he could solve the problem the images on the three monitors diverged. They pictured the same subject—a bespectacled male in his late twenties sitting in a chair—but each showed the scene from a different angle. One took in the subject full length and in profile; the second was a three-quarter medium-shot, angled from above; the third a straightforward close-up of the subject's head and shoulders, shot through the glass of the test chamber and from the front. The three images were in black and white, and none were completely centered or focused. Indeed, as the tapes began to run somebody was still adjusting such technicalities. A backwash of informal chatter ran between the subject and the woman—recognizable even in brief glimpses as the deceased—who was applying electrodes to his forehead. Much of the talk between them was difficult to catch; the acoustics in the chamber frustrated microphone and listener alike.

"The woman's Doctor Dance," Boyle offered. "The victim."

"Yes," said Carnegie, watching the screens intently, "I recognize her. How long does this preparation go on for?"

"Quite a while. Most of it's unedifying."

"Well, get to the edifying stuff, then."

"Fast forward," Boyle said. The technician obliged,

and the actors on the three screens became squeaking comedians. "Wait!" said Boyle. "Back up a short way." Again, the technician did as instructed. "There!" said Boyle. "Stop there. Now run on at normal speed." The action settled back to its natural pace. "This is where it really begins, sir."

Carnegie had come to the end of his hot chocolate. He put his finger into the soft sludge at the bottom of the cup, delivering the sickly-sweet dregs to his tongue. On the screens Doctor Dance had approached the subject with a syringe, was now swabbing the crook of his elbow, and injecting him. Not for the first time since his visit to the Hume Laboratories did Carnegie wonder precisely what they did at the establishment. Was this kind of procedure *de rigueur* in pharmaceutical research? The implicit secrecy of the experiment—late at night in an otherwise deserted building—suggested not. And there was that imperative on the title card—*"Restricted."* What they were watching had clearly never been intended for public viewing.

"Are you comfortable?" a man off camera now inquired. The subject nodded. His glasses had been removed and he looked slightly bemused without them. An unremarkable face, thought Carnegie; the subject—as yet unnamed—was neither Adonis nor Quasimodo. He was receding slightly, and his wispy, dirty-blond hair touched his shoulders.

"I'm fine, Doctor Welles," he replied to the off-camera questioner.

"You don't feel hot at all? Sweaty?"

"Not really," the guinea pig replied, slightly apologetically. "I feel ordinary."

That you are, Carnegie thought; then to Boyle: "Have you been through the tapes to the end?"

"No, sir," Boyle replied. "I thought you'd want to see them first. I only ran them as far as the injection."

"Any word from the hospital on Doctor Welles?"

"At the last call he was still comatose."

Carnegie grunted and returned his attention to the screens. Following the burst of action with the injection the tapes now settled into nonactivity: the three cameras fixed on their short-sighted subject with beady stares, the torpor occasionally interrupted by an inquiry from Welles as to the subject's condition. It remained the same. After three or four minutes of this eventless study even his occasional blinks began to assume major dramatic significance.

"Don't think much of the plot," the technician commented. Carnegie laughed; Boyle looked discomforted. Two or three more minutes passed in a similar manner.

"This doesn't look too hopeful," Carnegie said. "Run through it at speed, will you?"

The technician was about to obey when Boyle said: "Wait."

Carnegie glanced across at the man, irritated by his intervention, and then back at the screens. Something was happening. A subtle transformation had overtaken the insipid features of the subject. He had begun to smile to himself and was sinking down in his chair as if submerging his gangling body in a warm bath. His eyes, which had so far expressed little but affable indifference, now began to flicker closed, and then, once closed, opened again. When they did so there was a quality in them not previously visible, a hunger that seemed to reach out from the screen and into the calm of the inspector's office.

Carnegie put down his chocolate cup and approached the screens. As he did so the subject also got up out of his chair and walked toward the glass of the chamber, leaving two of the cameras' ranges. The third still recorded him, however, as he pressed his face against the window, and for a moment the two men faced each other through layers of glass and time, seemingly meeting each other's gaze.

The look on the man's face was critical now, the hunger was rapidly outgrowing sane control. Eyes burning, he laid his lips against the chamber window and kissed it, his tongue working against the glass.

"What in Christ's name is going on?" Carnegie said.

A prattle of voices had begun on the soundtrack. Doctor Welles was vainly asking the testee to articulate his feelings while Dance called off figures from the various monitoring instruments. It was difficult to hear much clearly—the din was further supplemented by an eruption of chatter from the caged monkeys—but it was evident that the readings coming through from the man's body were escalating. His face was flushed, his skin gleamed with a sudden sweat. He resembled a martyr with the tinder at his feet freshly lit, wild with a fatal ecstasy. He stopped French-kissing the window, tearing off the electrodes at his temples and the sensors from his arms and chest. Dance, her voice now registering alarm, called out for him to stop. Then she moved across the camera's view and out again crossing, Carnegie presumed, to the chamber door.

"Better not," he said, as if this drama were played out at his behest, and at a whim he could prevent the tragedy. But the woman took no notice. A moment later she appeared in long shot as she stepped into the chamber. The man moved to greet her, throwing over equipment as he did so. She called out to him—his name, perhaps. If so, it was inaudible over the monkeys' hullabaloo. "Shit," said Carnegie, as the testee's flailing arms caught first the profile camera, and then the three-quarter medium-shot. Two of the three monitors went dead. Only the head-on shot, the camera safe outside the chamber, still recorded events, but the tightness of the shot precluded more than an occasional glimpse of a moving body. Instead, the camera's sober eye gazed on, almost ironically, at the saliva smeared glass of the chamber window, blind to the atrocities being committed a few feet out of range.

"What in Christ's name did they give him?" Carnegie said, as somewhere off camera the woman's screams rose over the screeching of the apes.

Jerome woke in the early afternoon feeling hungry and sore. When he threw the sheet off his body he was appalled at his state. His torso was scored with scratches, and his groin region was red-raw. Wincing, he moved to the edge of the bed and sat there for a while, trying to piece the previous evening back together again. He remembered going to the laboratories, but very little after that. He had been a paid guinea pig for several months, giving of his blood, comfort and patience to supplement his meager earnings as a translator. The arrangement had begun courtesy of a friend who did similar work, but whereas Figley had been part of the laboratories' mainstream program, Jerome had been approached after one week at the place by Doctors

Welles and Dance, who had invited him—subject to a series of psychological tests—to work exclusively for them. It had been made clear from the outset that their project (he had never even been told its purpose) was of a secret nature, and that they would demand his total dedication and discretion. He had needed the funds, and the recompense they offered was marginally better than that paid by the laboratories, so he had agreed, although the hours they had demanded of him were unsociable. For several weeks now he had been required to attend the research facility late at night and often working into the small hours of the morning as he endured Welles's interminable questions about his private life and Dance's glassy stare.

Thinking of her cold look, he felt a tremor in him. Was it because once he had fooled himself that she had looked upon him more fondly than a doctor need? Such self-deception, he chided himself, was pitiful. He was not the stuff of which women dreamed, and each day he walked the streets reinforced that conviction. He could not remember one occasion in his adult life when a woman had looked his way, and kept looking; a time when an appreciative glance of his had been returned. Why this should bother him now he wasn't certain. His loveless condition was, he knew, commonplace. And nature had been kind. Knowing, it seemed, that the gift of allurement had passed him by, it had seen fit to minimize his libido. Weeks passed without his conscious thoughts mourning his enforced chastity.

Once in a while, when he heard the pipes roar, he might wonder what Mrs. Morrisey, his landlady, looked like in her bath; might imagine the firmness of her soapy breasts, or the dark divide of her rump as she stooped to put talcum powder between her toes. But such torments were, blissfully, infrequent. And when his cup brimmed he would pocket the money he had saved from his sessions at the laboratories and buy an hour's companionship from a woman called Angela (he'd never learned her second name) on Greek Street.

It would be several weeks before he did so again, he thought. Whatever he had done last night, or, more correctly, had done to him, the bruises alone had nearly crippled him. The only plausible explanation—though he couldn't recall any details—was that he'd been beaten up on the way back from the laboratories. Either that, or he'd stepped into a bar and somebody had picked a fight with him. It had happened before, on occasion. He had one of those faces that woke the bully in drunkards.

He stood up and hobbled to the small bathroom adjoining his room. His glasses were missing from their normal spot beside the shaving mirror and his reflection was woefully blurred, but it was apparent that his face was as badly scratched as the rest of his anatomy. And more: a clump of hair had been pulled out from above his left ear; clotted blood ran down to his neck. Painfully, he bent to the task of cleaning his wounds, then bathing them in a stinging solution of antiseptic. That done, he returned into his room to seek out his spectacles. But search as he might he could not locate them. Cursing his idiocy, he rooted among his belongings for his old pair and found them. Their prescription was out of date—his eyes had worsened considerably since he'd worn them—but they at least brought his surroundings into a dreamy kind of focus.

An indisputable melancholy had crept up on him,

compounded of his pain and those unwelcome thoughts of Mrs. Morrisey. To keep its intimacy at bay he turned on the radio. A sleek voice emerged, purveying the usual palliatives. Jerome had always had contempt for popular music and its apologists, but now, as he mooched around the small room, unwilling to clothe himself with chafing weaves when his scratches still pained him, the songs began to stir something other than scorn in him. It was as though he were hearing the words and music for the first time, as though all his life he had been deaf to their sentiments. Enthralled, he forgot his pain and listened. The songs told one seamless and obsessive story: of love lost and found, only to be lost again. The lyricists filled the airwaves with metaphor—much of it ludicrous, but no less potent for that. Of paradise, of hearts on fire; of birds, bells, journeys, sunsets; of passion as lunacy, as flight, as unimaginable treasure. The songs did not calm him with their fatuous sentiments. They flayed him, evoking, despite feeble rhyme and trite melody, a world bewitched by desire. He began to tremble. His eyes, strained (or so he reasoned) by the unfamiliar spectacles, began to delude him. It seemed as though he could see traces of light in his skin, sparks flying from the ends of his fingers.

He stared at his hands and arms. The illusion, far from retreating in the face of this scrutiny, increased. Beads of brightness, like the traces of fire in ash, began to climb through his veins, multiplying even as he watched. Curiously, he felt no distress. This burgeoning fire merely reflected the passion in the story the songs were telling him. Love, they said, was in the air, around every corner, waiting to be found. He thought again of the widow Morrisey in the flat below him, going about

her business, sighing, no doubt, as he had done; awaiting her hero. The more he thought of her the more in-
flamed he became. She would not reject him, of that the
songs convinced him. Or if she did he must press his
case until (again, as the songs promised) she surren-
dered to him. Suddenly, at the thought of her surrender,
the fire engulfed him. Laughing, he left the radio singing behind him and made his way downstairs.

It had taken the best part of the morning to assemble
a list of testees employed at the laboratories. Carnegie
had sensed a reluctance on the part of the establishment
to open their files to the investigation despite the horror
that had been committed on its premises. Finally, just
after noon, they had presented him with a hastily assembled who's who of subjects, four and a half dozen *in
toto*, and their addresses. None, the offices claimed,
matched the description of Welles's testee. The doctors,
it was explained, had been clearly using laboratory facilities to work on private projects. Though this was not
encouraged, both had been senior researchers, and allowed leeway on the matter. It was likely, therefore, that
the man Carnegie was seeking had never even been on
the laboratories' payroll. Undaunted, Carnegie ordered
a selection of photographs taken off the video recording
and had them distributed—with the list of names and
addresses—to his officers. From then on it was down to
footwork and patience.

Leo Boyle ran his finger down the list of names he
had been given. "Another fourteen," he said. His driver
grunted, and Boyle glanced across at him. "You were
McBride's partner, weren't you?" he said.

"That's right," Dooley replied. "He's been suspended."

"Why?"

Dooley scowled. "Lacks finesse, that Virgil. Can't get the hang of arrest technique."

Dooley drew the car to a halt.

"Is this it?" Boyle asked.

"You said number eighty. This is eighty. On the door. Eight. Oh."

"I've got eyes."

Boyle got out of the car and made his way up the pathway. The house was sizable, and had been divided into flats. There were several bells. He pressed for J. Tredgold—the name on his list—and waited. Of the five houses they had so far visited, two had been unoccupied and the residents of the other three had born no resemblance to the malefactor.

Boyle waited on the step a few seconds and then pressed the bell again; a longer ring this time.

"Nobody in," Dooley said from the pavement.

"Looks like it." Even as he spoke Boyle caught sight of a figure flitting across the hallway, its outline distorted by the cobblestone glass in the door. "Wait a minute," he said.

"What is it?"

"Somebody's in there and not answering." He pressed the first bell again, and then the others. Dooley approached up the pathway, flicking away an overattentive wasp.

"You sure?" he said.

"I saw somebody in there."

"Press the other bells," Dooley suggested.

"I already did. There's somebody in there and they

217

don't want to come to the door." He rapped on the glass. "Open up," he announced. "Police."

Clever, thought Dooley; why not a loudspeaker, so heaven knows too? When the door, predictably, remained unanswered, Boyle turned to Dooley. "Is there a side gate?"

"Yes, sir."

"Then get around the back, pronto, before he's away."

"Shouldn't we call——?"

"Do it? I'll keep watch here. If you can get in the back come through and open the front door."

Dooley moved, leaving Boyle alone at the front door. He rang the series of bells again and, cupping his hand to his brow, put his face to the glass. There was no sign of movement in the hallway. Was it possible that the bird had already flown? He backed down the path and stared up at the windows; they stared back vacuously. Ample time had now passed for Dooley to get around the back of the house, but so far he had neither reappeared nor called. Stymied where he stood, and nervous that his tactics had lost them their quarry, Boyle decided to follow his nose around the back of the house.

The side gate had been left open by Dooley. Boyle advanced up the side passage, glancing through a window into an empty living room before heading around to the back door. It was open. Dooley, however, was not in sight. Boyle pocketed the photograph and the list and stepped inside, loath to call Dooley's name for fear it alert any felon to his presence, yet nervous of the silence. Cautious as a cat on broken glass he crept through the flat, but each room was deserted. At the apartment door, which let on to the hallway in which he had first seen the figure, he paused. Where had Dooley gone? The man had apparently disappeared from sight.

Then, a groan from beyond the door.

"Dooley?" Boyle ventured. Another groan. He stepped into the hallway. Three more doors presented themselves, all were closed; other flats, presumably. On the coconut mat at the front door lay Dooley's truncheon, dropped there as if its owner had been in the process of making his escape. Boyle swallowed his fear and walked into the body of the hall. The complaint came again, close by. He looked around and up the stairs. There, on the half-landing, lay Dooley. He was barely conscious. A rough attempt had been made to rip his clothes. Large portions of his flabby lower anatomy were exposed.

"What's going on, Dooley?" Boyle asked, moving to the bottom of the stairs. The officer heard his voice and rolled himself over. His bleary eyes, settling on Boyle, opened in terror.

"It's all right," Boyle reassured him. "It's only me."

Too late, Boyle registered that Dooley's gaze wasn't fixed on *him* at all, but on some sight over his shoulder. As he pivoted on his heel to snatch a glance at Dooley's bugaboo a charging figure slammed into him. Winded and cursing, Boyle was thrown off his feet. He scrabbled about on the floor for several seconds before his attacker seized hold of him by jacket and hair and hauled him to his feet. He recognized at once the wild face that was thrust into his—the receding hairline, the weak mouth, the *hunger*—but there was much too he had not anticipated. For one, the man was naked as a babe, though scarcely so modestly endowed. For another, he was clearly aroused to fever pitch. If the beady eye at his groin, shining up at Boyle, were not evidence enough, the hands now tearing at his clothes made the assailant's intention perfectly apparent.

"Dooley!" Boyle shrieked as he was thrown across the hallway. "In Christ's name! Dooley!"

His pleas were silenced as he hit the opposite wall. The wild man was at his back in half a heartbeat, smearing Boyle's face against the wallpaper. Birds and flowers, intertwined, filled his eyes. In desperation Boyle fought back, but the man's passion lent him ungovernable strength. With one insolent hand holding the policeman's head, he tore at Boyle's trousers and underwear, leaving his buttocks exposed.

"God . . ." Boyle begged into the pattern of the wallpaper. "Please God, somebody help me . . ." But the prayers were no more fruitful than his struggles. He was pinned against the wall like a butterfly spread on cork, about to be pierced through. He closed his eyes, tears of frustration running down his cheeks. The assailant left off his hold on Boyle's head and pressed his violation home. Boyle refused to cry out. The pain he felt was not the equal of his shame. Better perhaps that Dooley remained comatose; that this humiliation be done and finished with unwitnessed.

"Stop," he murmured into the wall, not to his attacker but to his body, urging it not to find pleasure in this outrage. But his nerve endings were treacherous; they caught fire from the assault. Beneath the stabbing agony some unforgivable part of him rose to the occasion.

On the stairs, Dooley hauled himself to his feet. His lumbar region, which had been weak since the car accident the previous Christmas, had given out almost as soon as the wild man had sprung him in the hall. Now, as he descended the stairs, the least motion caused excruciating agonies. Crippled with pain he stumbled to the bottom of the stairs and looked, amazed, across the hallway. Could this be Boyle—he the supercilious, he the rising man, being pummeled like a street kid in need of dope money? The sight transfixed Dooley for several seconds before he unhinged his eyes and swung them down to the truncheon on the mat. He moved cautiously, but the wild man was too occupied with the deflowering to notice him.

Jerome was listening to Boyle's heart. It was a loud, seductive beat, and with every thrust into the man it seemed to get louder. He wanted it: the heat of it, the life of it. His hand moved around to Boyle's chest and dug at the flesh.

"Give me your heart," he said. It was like a line from one of the songs.

Boyle screamed into the wall as his attacker mauled his chest. He'd seen photographs of the woman at the laboratories; the open wound of her torso was lightning-clear in his mind's eye. Now the maniac intended the same atrocity. *Give me your heart.* Panicked to the ledge of his sanity he found new stamina and began to fight afresh, reaching around and clawing at the man's torso. Nothing—not even the bloody loss of hair from his scalp—broke the rhythm of his thrusts, however. In extremis, Boyle attempted to insinuate one of his hands between his body and the wall and reach between his legs to unman the bastard. As he did so, Dooley attacked, delivering a hail of truncheon blows upon the man's head. The diversion gave Boyle precious leeway. He pressed hard against the wall. The man, his grip on

Boyle's chest slicked with blood, lost his hold. Again, Boyle pushed. This time he managed to shrug the man off entirely. The bodies disengaged. Boyle turned, bleeding but in no danger, and watched Dooley follow the man across the hallway, beating at his greasy blond head. He made little attempt to protect himself however. His burning eyes (Boyle had never understood the physical accuracy of that image until now) were still on the object of his affections.

"Kill him!" Boyle said quietly as the man grinned—grinned!—through the blows. "Break every bone in his body!"

Even if Dooley, hobbled as he was, had been in any fit state to obey the imperative, he had no chance to do so. His berating was interrupted by a voice from down the hallway. A woman had emerged from the flat Boyle had come through. She too had been a victim of this marauder, to judge by her state. But Dooley's entry into the house had clearly distracted her molester before he could do serious damage.

"Arrest him!" she said, pointing at the leering man. "He tried to rape me!"

Dooley closed in to take possession of the prisoner, but Jerome had other intentions. He put his hand in Dooley's face and pushed him back against the front door. The coconut mat slid from under him; he all but fell. By the time he'd regained his balance Jerome was up and away. Boyle made a wretched attempt to stop him, but the tatters of his trousers were wrapped about his lower legs and Jerome, fleet-footed, was soon halfway up the stairs.

"Call for help," Boyle ordered Dooley. "And make it quick."

Dooley nodded and opened the front door.

"Is there any way out from upstairs?" Boyle demanded of Mrs. Morrisey. She shook her head. "Then we've got the bastard trapped, haven't we?" he said. "Go on, Dooley!" Dooley hobbled away down the path. "And you," he said to the woman, "fetch something in the way of weaponry. Anything solid." The woman nodded and returned the way she'd come, leaving Boyle slumped beside the open door. A soft breeze cooled the sweat on his face. At the car outside Dooley was calling up reinforcements.

All too soon, Boyle thought, the cars would be here, and the man upstairs would be hauled away to give his testimony. There would be no opportunity for revenge once he was in custody. The law would take its placid course, and he, the victim, would be only a bystander. If he was ever to salvage the ruins of his manhood, *now* was the time. If he didn't—if he languished here, his bowels on fire—he would never shrug off the horror he felt at his body's betrayal. He must act now—must beat the grin off his ravisher's face once and for all—or else live in self-disgust until memory failed him.

The choice was no choice at all. Without further debate, he got up from his squatting position and began up the stairs. As he reached the half-landing he realized he hadn't brought a weapon with him. He knew, however, that if he descended again he'd lose all momentum. Prepared, in that moment, to die if necessary, he headed on up.

There was only one door open on the top landing. Through it came the sound of a radio. Downstairs, in the safety of the hall, he heard Dooley come in to tell him that the call had been made, only to break off in mid-announcement. Ignoring the distraction, Boyle stepped into the flat.

There was nobody there. It took Boyle a few moments only to check the kitchen, the tiny bathroom and the living room. All were deserted. He returned to the bathroom, the window of which was open, and put his head out. The drop to the grass of the garden below was quite manageable. There was an imprint in the ground of the man's body. He had leaped. And gone.

Boyle cursed his tardiness and hung his head. A trickle of heat ran down the inside of his leg. In the next room, the love songs played on.

For Jerome, there was no forgetfulness, not this time. The encounter with Mrs. Morrisey, which had been interrupted by Dooley, and the episode with Boyle that had followed, had all merely served to fan the fire in him. Now, by the light of those flames, he saw clearly what crimes he had committed. He remembered with horrible clarity the laboratory, the injection, the monkeys, the blood. The acts he recalled, however (and there were many), woke no sense of sinfulness in him. All moral consequence, all shame or remorse, was burned out by the fire that was even now licking his flesh to new enthusiasms.

He took refuge in a quiet cul-de-sac to make himself presentable. The clothes he had managed to snatch before making his escape were motley but would serve to keep him from attracting unwelcome attention. As he buttoned himself up—his body seeming to strain from its covering as if resentful of being concealed—he tried to control the holocaust that raged between his ears. But the flames wouldn't be dampened. His every fiber seemed alive to the flux and flow of the world around him. The marshaled trees along the road, the wall at his back, the very paving stones beneath his bare feet were catching a spark from him and burning now with their own fire. He grinned to see the conflagration spread. The world, in its every eager particular, grinned back.

Aroused beyond control, he turned to the wall he had been leaning against. The sun had fallen full upon it, and it was warm; the bricks smelled ambrosial. He laid kisses on their gritty faces, his hands exploring every nook and cranny. Murmuring sweet nothings, he unzipped himself, found an accommodating niche, and filled it. His mind was running with liquid pictures: mingled anatomies, female and male in one undistinguishable congress. Above him, even the clouds had caught fire. Enthralled by their burning heads he felt the moment rise in his gristle. Breath was short now. But the ecstasy? Surely that would go on forever.

Without warning a spasm of pain traveled down his spine from cortex to testicles and back again, convulsing him. His hands lost grip of the brick and he finished his agonizing climax on the air as he fell across the pavement. For several seconds he lay where he had collapsed, while the echoes of the initial spasm bounced back and forth along his spine, diminishing with each return. He could taste blood at the back of his throat. He wasn't certain if he'd bitten his lip or tongue, but he thought not. Above his head the birds circled on, rising lazily on a spiral of warm air. He watched the fire in the clouds gutter out.

He got to his feet and looked down at the coinage of semen he'd spent on the pavement. For a fragile instant he caught again a whiff of the vision he'd just had;

imagined a marriage of his seed with the paving stone. What sublime children the world might boast, he thought, if he could only mate with brick or tree. He would gladly suffer the agonies of conception if such miracles were possible. But the paving stone was unmoved by his seed's entreaties. The vision, like the fire above him, cooled and hid its glories.

He put his bloodied member away and leaned against the wall, turning the strange events of his recent life over and over. Something fundamental was changing in him, of that he had no doubt. The rapture that had possessed him (and would, no doubt, possess him again) was like nothing he had hitherto experienced. And whatever they had injected into his system, it showed no signs of being discharged naturally; far from it. He could feel the heat in him still, as he had leaving the laboratories, but this time the roar of its presence was louder than ever.

It was a new kind of life he was living, and the thought, though frightening, exulted him. Not once did it occur to his spinning, eroticized brain that this new kind of life would, in time, demand a new kind of death.

Carnegie had been warned by his superiors that results were expected. He was now passing the verbal beating he'd received to those under him. It was a line of humiliation in which the greater was encouraged to kick the lesser man, and that man, in turn, his lesser. Carnegie had sometimes wondered what the man at the end of the line took his ire out on; his dog presumably.

"This miscreant is still loose, gentlemen, despite his photograph in many of this morning's newspapers and an operating method which is, to say the least, insolent. We *will* catch him, of course, but let's get the bastard before we have another murder on our hands—"

The phone rang. Boyle's replacement, Migeon, picked it up, while Carnegie concluded his pep talk to the assembled officers.

"I want him in the next twenty-four hours, gentlemen. That's the time scale I've been given, and that's what we've got. Twenty-four hours."

Migeon interrupted. "Sir? It's Johannson. He says he's got something for you. It's urgent."

"Right." The inspector claimed the receiver. "Carnegie."

The voice at the other end was soft to the point of inaudibility. "Carnegie," Johannson said, "we've been right through the laboratory, dug up every piece of information we could find on Dance and Welles's tests—"

"And?"

"We've also analyzed traces of the agent from the hypo they used on the suspect. I think we've found the *Boy,* Carnegie."

"What boy?" Carnegie wanted to know. He found Johannson's obfuscation irritating.

"The Blind Boy, Carnegie."

"And?"

For some inexplicable reason Carnegie was certain the man *smiled* down the phone before replying: "I think perhaps you'd better come down and see for yourself. Sometime around noon suit you?"

Johannson could have been one of history's greatest poisoners. He had all the requisite qualifications. A tidy mind (poisoners were, in Carnegie's experience, domestic paragons), a patient nature (poison could take time) and, most importantly, an encyclopedic knowledge of toxicology. Watching him at work, which Carnegie had done on two previous cases, was to see a subtle man at his subtle craft, and the spectacle made Carnegie's blood run cold.

Johannson had installed himself in the laboratory on the top floor, where Doctor Dance had been murdered, rather than use police facilities for the investigation, because, as he explained to Carnegie, much of the equipment the Hume organization boasted was simply not available elsewhere. His dominion over the place, accompanied by his two assistants, had, however, transformed the laboratory from the clutter left by the experimenters to a dream of order. Only the monkeys remained a constant. Try as he might Johannson could not control their behavior.

"We didn't have much difficulty finding the drug used on your man," Johannson said, "we simply cross-checked traces remaining in the hypodermic with materials found in the room. In fact, they seem to have been manufacturing this stuff, or variations on the theme, for some time. The people here claim they know nothing about it, of course. I'm inclined to believe them. What the good doctors were doing here was, I'm sure, in the nature of a personal experiment."

"What sort of experiment?"

Johannson took off his spectacles and set about cleaning them with the tongue of his red tie. "At first, we thought they were developing some kind of hallucinogen," he said. "In some regards the agent used on your man resembles a narcotic. In fact—methods apart

—I think they made some very exciting discoveries. Developments which take us into entirely new territory."

"It's not a drug then?"

"Oh, yes, of course it's a drug," Johannson said, replacing the spectacles, "but one created for a very specific purpose. See for yourself."

Johannson led the way across the laboratory to the row of monkeys' cages. Instead of being confined separately, the toxicologist had seen fit to open the interconnecting doors between one cage and the next, allowing the animals free access to gather in groups. The consequence was absolutely plain—the animals were engaged in an elaborate series of sexual acts. Why, Carnegie wondered, did monkeys perpetually perform obscenities? It was the same torrid display whenever he'd taken his offspring, as children, to Regent's Park Zoo; the ape enclosure elicited one embarrassing question upon another. He'd stopped taking the children after a while. He simply found it too mortifying.

"Haven't they got anything better to do?" he asked of Johannson, glancing away and then back at a menage à trois that was so intimate the eye could not ascribe member to monkey.

"Believe me," Johannson smirked, "this is mild by comparison with much of the behavior we've seen from them since we gave them a shot of the agent. From that point on they neglected all normal behavior patterns. They bypassed the arousal signals, the courtship rituals. They no longer show any interest in food. They don't sleep. They have become sexual obsessives. All other stimuli are forgotten. Unless the agent is naturally discharged, I suspect they are going to screw themselves to death."

Carnegie looked along the rest of the cages. The same pornographic scenes were being played out in each one. Mass rape, homosexual liaisons, fervent and ecstatic masturbation.

"It's no wonder the doctors made a secret project of their discovery," Johannson went on. "They were on to something that could have made them a fortune. An aphrodisiac that actually works."

"An aphrodisiac?"

"Most are useless, of course. Rhinoceros horn, live eels in cream sauce: symbolic stuff. They're designed to arouse by association."

Carnegie remembered the hunger in Jerome's eyes. It was echoed here in the monkeys'. Hunger, and the desperation that hunger brings.

"And the ointments too, all useless. *Cantharis vesticatora—*"

"What's that?"

"You know the stuff as Spanish fly, perhaps? It's a paste made from a beetle. Again, useless. At best these things are irritants. But this . . ." He picked up a vial of colorless fluid. *"This* is damn near genius."

"They don't look too happy with it to me."

"Oh, it's still crude," Johannson said. "I think the researchers were greedy and moved into tests on living subjects a good two or three years before it was wise to do so. The stuff is almost lethal as it stands, no doubt of that. But it *could* be made to work, given time. You see, they've sidestepped the mechanical problems. This stuff operates directly on the sexual imagination, on the libido. If you arouse the *mind,* the body follows. That's the trick of it."

A rattling of the wire mesh close by drew Carnegie's

attention from Johannson's pale features. One of the female monkeys, apparently not satisfied with the attentions of several males, was spread-eagled against her cage, her nimble fingers reaching for Carnegie. Her spouses, not to be left loveless, had taken to sodomy. *"Blind Boy?"* said Carnegie. "Is that Jerome?"

"It's Cupid, isn't it?" Johannson said:

> *"Love looks not with the eyes but with the mind,*
> *And therefore is winged Cupid painted blind.*

It's *Midsummer Night's Dream."*

"The bard was never my strongest suit," said Carnegie. He went back to staring at the female monkey. "And Jerome?" he said.

"He has the agent in his system. A sizable dose."

"So he's like this lot!"

"I would presume—his intellectual capacities being greater—that the agent may not be able to work in quite such an *unfettered* fashion. But, having said that, sex can make monkeys out of the best of us, can't it?" Johannson allowed himself a half-smile at the notion. "All our so-called higher concerns become secondary to the pursuit. For a short time sex makes us obsessive. We can perform, or at least *think* we can perform, what with hindsight may seem extraordinary feats."

"I don't think there's anything so extraordinary about rape," Carnegie commented, attempting to stem Johannson's rhapsody. But the other man would not be subdued.

"Sex without end, without compromise or apology," he said. "Imagine it. The dream of Casanova."

* * *

The world had seen so many Ages: the Age of Enlightenment; of Reformation; of Reason. Now, at last, the Age of Desire. And after this, an end to Ages; an end, perhaps, to everything. For the fires that were being stoked now were fiercer than the innocent world suspected. They were terrible fires, fires without end, which would illuminate the world in one last, fierce light.

So Welles thought as he lay in his bed. He had been conscious for several hours, but had chosen not to signify such. Whenever a nurse came to his room he would clamp his eyes closed and slow the rhythm of his breath. He knew he could not keep the illusion up for long, but the hours gave him a while to think through his itinerary from here. His first move had to be back to the laboratories. There were papers there he had to shred, tapes to wipe clean. From now on he was determined that every scrap of information about *Project Blind Boy* exist solely in his head. That way he would have complete control over his masterwork, and nobody could claim it from him.

He had never had much interest in making money from the discovery, although he was well aware of how lucrative a workable aphrodisiac would be; he had never given a fig for material wealth. His initial motivation for the development of the drug—which they had chanced upon quite by accident while testing an agent to aid schizophrenics—had been investigative. But his motives had matured through their months of secret work. He had come to think of himself as the bringer of the millennium. He would not have anyone attempt to snatch that sacred role from him.

So he thought, lying in his bed, waiting for a moment to slip away.

As he walked the streets Jerome would have happily affirmed Welles's vision. Perhaps he, of all men, was most eager to welcome the Age of Desire. He saw its portents everywhere: on advertising billboards and cinema marquees, in shop windows, on television screens —everywhere, the body as merchandise. Where flesh was not being used to market artifacts of steel and stone, those artifacts were taking on its properties. Automobiles passed him by with every voluptuous attribute but breath—their sinuous bodywork gleamed, their interiors invited plushly. The buildings beleaguered him with sexual puns: spires, passageways, shadowed plazas with white-water fountains. Beneath the raptures of the shallow—the thousand trivial distractions he encountered in street and square—he sensed the ripe life of the body informing every particular.

The spectacle kept the fire in him well stoked. It was all that will power could do to keep him from pressing his attentions on every creature that he met eyes with. A few seemed to sense the heat in him and gave him wide berth. Dogs sensed it too. Several followed him, aroused by *his* arousal. Flies orbited his head in squadrons. But his growing ease with his condition gave him some rudimentary control over it. He knew that to make a public display of his ardor would bring the law down upon him, and that in turn would hinder his adventures. Soon enough, the fire that he had begun would spread. *Then* he would emerge from hiding and bathe in it freely. Until then, discretion was best.

He had on occasion bought the company of a young

woman in Soho; he went to find her now. The afternoon was stiflingly hot, but he felt no weariness. He had not eaten since the previous evening, but he felt no hunger. Indeed, as he climbed the narrow stairway up to the room on the first floor which Angela had once occupied, he felt as primed as an athlete, glowing with health. The immaculately dressed and wall-eyed pimp who usually occupied a place at the top of the stairs was absent. Jerome simply went to the girl's room and knocked. There was no reply. He rapped again, more urgently. The noise brought an early middle-aged woman to the door at the end of the landing.

"What do you want?"

"The woman," he replied simply.

"Angela's gone. And you'd better get out of here too in that state. This isn't a flophouse."

"When will she be back?" he asked, keeping as tight a leash as he could on his appetite.

The woman, who was as tall as Jerome and half as heavy again as his wasted frame, advanced toward him. "The girl won't *be* back," she said, "so you get the hell out of here, before I call Isaiah."

Jerome looked at the woman. She shared Angela's profession, no doubt, if not her youth or prettiness. He smiled at her. "I can hear your heart," he said.

"I told you—"

Before she could finish the words Jerome moved down the landing toward her. She wasn't intimidated by his approach, merely repulsed.

"If I call Isaiah, you'll be sorry," she informed him. The pace of her heartbeat had risen, he could hear it.

"I'm burning," he said.

She frowned. She was clearly losing this battle of

wits. "Stay away from me," she said. "I'm warning you."

The heartbeat was getting more rapid still. The rhythm, buried in her substance, drew him on. From that source: all life, all heat.

"Give me your heart," he said.

"Isaiah!"

Nobody came running at her shout, however. Jerome gave her no opportunity to cry out a second time. He reached to embrace her, clamping a hand over her mouth. She let fly a volley of blows against him, but the pain only fanned the flames. He was brighter by the moment. His every orifice let onto the furnace in belly and loins and head. Her superior bulk was of no advantage against such fervor. He pushed her against the wall —the beat of her heart loud in his ears—and began to apply kisses to her neck, tearing her dress open to free her breasts.

"Don't shout," he said, trying to sound persuasive. "There's no harm meant."

She shook her head and said, "I won't," against his palm. He took his hand from her mouth and she dragged in several desperate breaths. Where was Isaiah? she thought. Not far, surely. Fearing for her life if she tried to resist this interloper—how his eyes shone!—she gave up any pretense to resistance and let him have his way. Men's supply of passion, she knew from long experience, was easily depleted. Though they might threaten to move earth and heaven too, half an hour later their boasts would be damp sheets and resentment. If worst came to worst, she could tolerate his inane talk of burning; she'd heard far obscener bedroom chat. As to the prong he was even now attempting to press into her, it and its comical like held no surprises for her.

Jerome wanted to touch the heart in her, wanted to see it splash up into his face, to bathe in it. He put his hand to her breast and felt the beat of her under his palm.

"You like that, do you?" she said as he pressed against her bosom. "You're not the first."

He clawed her skin.

"Gently, sweetheart," she chided him, looking over his shoulder to see if there was any sign of Isaiah. "Be gentle. This is the only body I've got."

He ignored her. His nails drew blood.

"Don't do that," she said.

"Wants to be out," he replied digging deeply, and it suddenly dawned on her that this was no love-game he was playing.

"*Stop it*," she said, as he began to tear at her. This time she screamed.

Downstairs, and a short way along the street, Isaiah dropped the slice of *tarte française* he'd just bought and ran to the door. It wasn't the first time his sweet tooth had tempted him from his post, but—unless he was quick to undo the damage—it might very well be his last. There were terrible noises from the landing. He raced up the stairs. The scene that met his eyes was in every way worse than that his imagination had conjured. Simone was trapped against the wall beside her door with a man battened upon her. Blood was coming from somewhere between them, he couldn't see where.

Isaiah yelled. Jerome, hands bloody, looked around from his labors as a giant in a Savile Row suit reached for him. It took Jerome vital seconds to uproot himself from the furrow, by which time the man was upon him. Isaiah took hold of him, and dragged him off the woman. She took shelter, sobbing, in her room.

"Sick bastard," Isaiah said, launching a fusillade of punches. Jerome reeled. But he was on fire, and unafraid. In a moment's respite he leaped at his man like an angered baboon. Isaiah, taken unawares, lost balance, and fell back against one of the doors, which opened inward against his weight. He collapsed into a squalid lavatory, his head striking the lip of the toilet bowl as he went down. The impact disoriented him, and he lay on the stained linoleum groaning, legs akimbo. Jerome could hear his blood, eager in his veins; could smell sugar on his breath. It tempted him to stay. But his instinct for self-preservation counseled otherwise; Isaiah was already making an attempt to stand up again. Before he could get to his feet Jerome turned about and made a getaway down the stairs.

The dog day met him at the doorstep, and he smiled. The street wanted him more than the woman on the landing, and he was eager to oblige. He started out onto the pavement, his erection still pressing from his trousers. Behind him he heard the giant pounding down the stairs. He took to his heels, laughing. The fire was still uncurbed in him, and it lent speed to his feet. He ran down the street not caring if Sugar Breath was following or not. Pedestrians, unwilling in this dispassionate age to register more than casual interest in the blood-spattered satyr, parted to let him pass. A few pointed, assuming him an actor perhaps. Most took no notice at all. He made his way through a maze of back streets, aware without needing to look that Isaiah was still on his heels.

Perhaps it was accident that brought him to the street market; perhaps, and more probably, it was that the swelter carried the mingled scent of meat and fruit to his nostrils and he wanted to bathe in it. The narrow thoroughfare was thronged with purchasers, sightseers and stalls heaped with merchandise. He dove into the crowd happily, brushing against buttock and thigh, meeting the plaguing gaze of fellow flesh on every side. Such a day! He and his prick could scarcely believe their luck.

Behind him he heard Isaiah shout. He picked up his pace, heading for the most densely populated area of the market, where he could lose himself in the hot press of people. Each contact was a painful ecstasy. Each climax—and they came one upon the other as he pressed through the crowd—was a dry spasm in his system. His back ached, his balls ached. But what was his body now? Just a plinth for that singular monument, his prick. Head was *nothing;* mind was *nothing*. His arms were simply made to bring love close, his legs to carry the demanding rod any place where it might find satisfaction. He pictured himself as a walking erection, the world gaping on every side. Flesh, brick, steel, he didn't care—he would ravish it all.

Suddenly, without his seeking it, the crowd parted, and he found himself off the main thoroughfare and in a narrow street. Sunlight poured between the buildings, its zeal magnified. He was about to turn back to join the crowd again when he caught a scent and sight that drew him on. A short way down the heat-drenched street three shirtless young men were standing amid piles of fruit crates, each containing dozens of baskets of strawberries. There had been a glut of the fruit that year, and in the relentless heat much of it had begun to soften and rot. The trio of workers was going through the baskets, sorting bad fruit from good, and throwing the spoiled strawberries into the gutter. The smell in the narrow space was overpowering, a sweetness of such strength it would have sickened any interloper other than Jerome, whose senses had lost all capacity for revulsion or rejection. The world was the world was the world; he would take it, as in marriage, for better or worse. He stood watching the spectacle entranced: the sweating fruit sorters bright in the fall of sun, hands, arms and torsos spattered with scarlet juice; the air mazed with every nectar-seeking insect; the discarded fruit heaped in the gutter in seeping mounds. Engaged in their sticky labors, the sorters didn't even see him at first. Then one of the three looked up and took in the extraordinary creature watching them. The grin on his face died as he met Jerome's eyes.

"What the hell?"

Now the other two looked up from their work.

"Sweet," said Jerome. He could hear their hearts tremble.

"Look at him," said the youngest of the three, pointing at Jerome's groin. "Fucking exposing himself."

They stood still in the sunlight, he and they, while the wasps whirled around the fruit and, in the narrow slice of blue summer sky between the roofs, birds passed over. Jerome wanted the moment to go on forever; his too-naked head tasted Eden here.

And then, the dream broke. He felt a shadow on his back. One of the sorters dropped the basket he was sorting through; the decayed fruit broke open on the gravel. Jerome frowned and half-turned. Isaiah had found the street. His weapon was steel and shone. It crossed the space between him and Jerome in one short second. Jerome felt an ache in his side as the knife slid into him.

"Christ," the young man said and began to run. His two brothers, unwilling to be witnesses at the scene of a wounding, hesitated only moments longer before following.

The pain made Jerome cry out, but nobody in the noisy market heard him. Isaiah withdrew the blade; heat came with it. He made to stab again but Jerome was too fast for the spoiler. He moved out of range and staggered across the street. The would-be assassin, fearful that Jerome's cries would draw too much attention, moved quickly in pursuit to finish the job. But the tarmac was slick with rotted fruit, and his fine suede shoes had less grip than Jerome's bare feet. The gap between them widened by a pace.

"No you don't," Isaiah said, determined not to let his humiliator escape. He pushed over a tower of fruit crates—baskets toppled and strewed their contents across Jerome's path. Jerome hesitated, to take in the bouquet of bruised fruit. The indulgence almost killed him. Isaiah closed in, ready to take the man. Jerome, his system taxed to near eruption by the stimulus of pain, watched the blade come close to opening up his belly. His mind conjured the wound: the abdomen slit—the heat spilling out to join the blood of the strawberries in the gutter. The thought was so tempting. He almost wanted it.

Isaiah had killed before, twice. He knew the wordless vocabulary of the act, and he could see the invitation in his victim's eyes. Happy to oblige, he came to meet it, knife at the ready. At the last possible moment Jerome recanted, and instead of presenting himself for slitting, threw a blow at the giant. Isaiah ducked to avoid it and his feet slid in the mush. The knife fled from his hand and fell among the debris of baskets and fruit. Jerome turned away as the hunter—the advantage lost—stooped to locate the knife. But his prey was gone before his ham-fisted grip had found it; lost again in the crowd-filled streets. He had no opportunity to pocket the knife before the uniform stepped out of the crowd and joined him in the hot passageway.

"What's the story?" the policeman demanded, looking down at the knife. Isaiah followed his gaze. The bloodied blade was black with flies.

In his office Inspector Carnegie sipped at his hot chocolate, his third in the past hour, and watched the processes of dusk. He had always wanted to be a detective, right from his earliest rememberings. And, in those rememberings, this had always been a charged and magical hour. Night descending on the city; myriad evils putting on their glad rags and coming out to play. A time for vigilance, for a new moral stringency.

But as a child he had failed to imagine the fatigue that twilight invariably brought. He was tired to his bones, and if he snatched any sleep in the next few hours he knew it would be here, in his chair, with his feet up on the desk amid a clutter of plastic cups.

The phone rang. It was Johannson.

"Still at work?" he said, impressed by Johannson's dedication to the job. It was well after nine. Perhaps Johannson didn't have a home worth calling such to go back to either.

"I heard our man had a busy day," Johannson said.

"That's right. A prostitute in Soho, then got himself stabbed."

"He got through the cordon, I gather?"

"These things happen," Carnegie replied, too tired to be testy. "What can I do for you?"

"I just thought you'd want to know: the monkeys have started to die."

The words stirred Carnegie from his fatigue-stupor. "How many?" he asked.

"Three from fourteen so far. But the rest will be dead by dawn, I'd guess."

"What's killing them? Exhaustion?" Carnegie recalled the desperate saturnalia he'd seen in the cages. What animal—human or otherwise—could keep up such revelry without cracking up?

"It's not physical," Johannson said. "Or at least not in the way you're implying. We'll have to wait for the dissection results before we get any detailed explanations—"

"Your best guess?"

"For what it's worth . . ." Johannson said, ". . . which is quite a lot: I think they're going *bang*."

"What?"

"Cerebral overload of some kind. Their brains are simply giving out. The agent doesn't disperse you see. *It feeds on itself*. The more fevered they get, the more of the drug is produced; the more of the drug there is, the more fevered they get. It's a vicious circle. Hotter and hotter, wilder and wilder. Eventually the system can't take it, and suddenly I'm up to my armpits in dead monkeys." The smile came back into the voice again, cold and wry. "Not that the others let that spoil their fun. Necrophilia's quite the fashion down here."

242

Carnegie peered at his cooling hot chocolate. It had acquired a thin skin which puckered as he touched the cup. "So it's just a matter of time?" he said.

"Before our man goes for bust? Yes, I'd think so."

"All right. Thank you for the update. Keep me posted."

"You want to come down here and view the remains?"

"Monkey corpses I can do without, thank you."

Johannson laughed. Carnegie put down the receiver. When he turned back to the window, night had well and truly fallen.

In the laboratory Johannson crossed to the light switch by the door. In the time he'd been calling Carnegie the last of the daylight had fled. He saw the blow that felled him coming a mere heartbeat before it landed; it caught him across the side of his neck. One of his vertebrae snapped and his legs buckled. He collapsed without reaching the light switch. But by the time he hit the ground the distinction between day and night was academic.

Welles didn't bother to check whether his blow had been lethal or not; time was at a premium. He stepped over the body and headed across to the bench where Johannson had been working. There, lying in a circle of lamplight as if for the final act of a simian tragedy, lay a dead monkey. It had clearly perished in a frenzy. Its face was knitted up; mouth wide and spittle-stained; eyes fixed in a final look of alarm. Its fur had been pulled out in tufts in the throes of its copulations. Its body, wasted with exertion, was a mass of contusions. It took Welles half a minute of study to recognize the implications of the corpse, and of the other two he now saw lying on a nearby bench.

"Love kills," he murmured to himself philosophically and began his systematic destruction of *Blind Boy*.

I'm dying, Jerome thought. I'm dying of *terminal joy*. The thought amused him. It was the only thought in his head which made much sense. Since his encounter with Isaiah and the escape from the police that had followed, he could remember little with any coherence. The hours of hiding and nursing his wounds—of feeling the heat grow again, and of discharging it—had long since merged into one midsummer dream, from which, he knew with pleasurable certainty, only death would wake him. The blaze was devouring him utterly, from the entrails out. If he were to be eviscerated now, what would the witnesses find? Only embers and ashes.

Yet still his one-eyed friend demanded *more*. Still, as he wove his way back to the laboratories—where else for a made man to go when the stitches slipped but back to the first heat?—still the grids gaped at him seductively, and every brick wall offered up a hundred gritty invitations.

The night was balmy: a night for love songs and romance. In the questionable privacy of a parking lot a few blocks from his destination he saw two people having sex in the back of a car, the doors open to accommodate limbs and draft. Jerome paused to watch the ritual, enthralled as ever by the tangle of bodies and the sound —so loud it was like thunder—of twin hearts beating to one escalating rhythm. Watching, his rod grew eager.

The female saw him first and alerted her partner to the wreck of a human being who was watching them with such childish delight. The male looked around from his gropings to stare. Do I burn, Jerome wondered? Does my hair flame? At the last, does the illusion gain substance? To judge by the look on their faces, the answer was surely no. They were not in awe of him, merely angered and revolted.

"I'm on fire," he told them.

The male got to his feet and spat at Jerome. He almost expected the spittle to turn to steam as it approached him but instead it landed on his face and upper chest as a cooling shower.

"Go to hell," the woman said. "Leave us alone."

Jerome shook his head. The male warned him that another step would oblige him to break Jerome's head. It disturbed our man not a jot; no words, no blows, could silence the imperative of the rod.

Their hearts, he realized, as he moved toward them, no longer beat in tandem.

Carnegie consulted the map, five years out of date now, on his office wall to pinpoint the location of the attack that had just been reported. Neither of the victims had come to serious harm, apparently. The arrival of a carload of revelers had dissuaded Jerome (it was unquestionably Jerome) from lingering. Now the area was being flooded with officers, half a dozen of them armed. In a matter of minutes every street in the vicinity of the attack would be cordoned off. Unlike Soho, which had been crowded, the area would furnish the fugitive with few hiding places.

Carnegie pinpointed the location of the attack and realized that it was within a few blocks of the laboratories. No accident, surely. The man was heading back to the scene of his crime. Wounded, and undoubtedly on the verge of collapse—the lovers had described a man who looked more dead than alive—Jerome would probably be picked up before he reached home. But there was always the risk of his slipping through the net and getting to the laboratories. Johannson was working there, alone. The guard on the building was, in these straitened times, necessarily small.

Carnegie picked up the phone and dialed through to Johannson. The phone rang at the other end but nobody picked it up. The man's gone home, Carnegie thought, happy to be relieved of his concern. It's ten-fifty at night and he's earned his rest. Just as he was about to put the receiver down, however, it was picked up at the other end.

"Johannson?"

Nobody replied.

"Johannson? This is Carnegie." And still, no reply. "Answer me, damn it. Who is this?"

In the laboratories the receiver was forsaken. It was not replaced on the cradle but left to lie on the bench. Down the buzzing line, Carnegie could clearly hear the monkeys, their voices shrill.

"Johannson?" Carnegie demanded. "Are you there? Johannson?"

But the apes screamed on.

Welles had built two bonfires of the *Blind Boy* material in the sinks and then set them alight. They flared up enthusiastically. Smoke, heat and ashes filled the large room, thickening the air. When the fires were fairly raging he threw all the tapes he could lay hands upon into the conflagration, and added all of Johannson's notes for good measure. Several of the tapes had already gone from the files, he noted. But all they could show any thief was some teasing scenes of transformation. The heart of the secret remained his. With the procedures and formulae now destroyed, it only remained to wash the small amounts of remaining agent down the drain and kill and incinerate the animals.

He prepared a series of lethal hypodermics, going about the business with uncharacteristic orderliness. This systematic destruction gratified him. He felt no regret at the way things had turned out. From that first moment of panic, when he'd helplessly watched the *Blind Boy* serum work its awesome effects upon Jerome, to this final elimination of all that had gone before had been, he now saw, one steady process of wiping clean. With these fires he brought an end to the pretense of scientific inquiry. After this he was indisputably the Apostle of Desire, its John in the Wilderness. The thought blinded him to any other. Careless of the monkeys' scratchings he hauled them one by one from their cages to deliver the killing dose. He had dispatched three, and was opening the cage of the fourth, when a figure appeared in the doorway of the laboratory. Through the smoky air it was impossible to see who. The surviving monkeys seemed to recognize him, however. They left off their couplings and set up a din of welcome.

Welles stood still and waited for the newcomer to make his move.

"I'm dying," said Jerome.

Welles had not expected this. Of all the people he had anticipated here, Jerome was the last.

"Did you hear me?" the man wanted to know.

Welles nodded. "We're *all* dying, Jerome. Life is a slow disease, no more nor less. But such a *light*, eh? in the going."

"You *knew* this would happen," Jerome said. "You knew the fire would eat me away."

"No," came the sober reply. "No, I didn't. Really."

Jerome walked out of the door frame and into the murky light. He was a wasted shambles, a patchwork man, blood on his body, fire in his eyes. But Welles knew better than to trust the apparent vulnerability of this scarecrow. The agent in his system had made him capable of superhuman acts. He had seen Dance torn open with a few nonchalant strokes. Tact was required. Though clearly close to death, Jerome was still formidable.

"I didn't intend this, Jerome," Welles said, attempting to tame the tremor in his voice. "I wish, in a way, I could claim that I had. But I wasn't that farsighted. It's taken me time and pain to see the future plainly."

The burning man watched him, gaze intent.

"Such fires, Jerome, waiting to be lit."

"I know . . ." Jerome replied. "Believe me . . . I know."

"You and I, we are the end of the world."

The wretched monster pondered this for a while, and then nodded slowly. Welles softly exhaled a sigh of relief. The deathbed diplomacy was working. But he had little time to waste with talk. If Jerome was here, could the authorities be far behind?

"I have urgent work to do, my friend," he said calmly. "Would you think me uncivil if I continued with it?"

Without waiting for a reply he unlatched another

cage and hauled the condemned monkey out, expertly turning its body around to facilitate the injection. The animal convulsed in his arms for a few moments, then died. Welles disengaged its wizened fingers from his shirt and tossed the corpse and the discharged hypodermic on to the bench, turning with an executioner's economy to claim his next victim.

"Why?" Jerome asked, staring at the animal's open eyes.

"Act of mercy," Welles replied, picking up another primed hypodermic. "You can see how they're suffering." He reached to unlatch the next cage.

"Don't," Jerome said.

"No time for sentiment," Welles replied. "I beg you, an end to that."

Sentiment, Jerome thought, muddily remembering the songs on the radio that had first rewoken the fire in him. Didn't Welles understand that the processes of heart and head and groin were indivisible? That sentiment, however trite, might lead to undiscovered regions? He wanted to tell the doctor that, to explain all that he had seen and all that he had loved in these desperate hours. But somewhere between mind and tongue the explanations absconded. All he could say, to state the empathy he felt for all the suffering world, was: *"Don't,"* as Welles unlocked the next cage. The doctor ignored him and reached into the wire-mesh cell. It contained three animals. He took hold of the nearest and drew it, protesting, from its companions' embraces. Without doubt it knew what fate awaited it; a flurry of screeches signaled its terror.

Jerome couldn't stomach this casual disposal. He moved, the wound in his side a torment, to prevent the killing. Welles, distracted by Jerome's advance, lost hold of his wriggling charge. The monkey scampered away across the benchtops. As he went to recapture it the prisoners in the cage behind him took their chance and slipped out.

"Damn you," Welles yelled at Jerome, "don't you see we've no *time?* Don't you understand?"

Jerome understood everything, and yet nothing. The fever he and the animals shared he understood; its purpose, to transform the world, he understood too. But why it should end like this—that joy, that vision—why it should all come down to a sordid room filled with smoke and pain, to frailty, to despair? *That* he did not comprehend. Nor, he now realized, did Welles, who had been the architect of these contradictions.

As the doctor made a snatch for one of the escaping monkeys, Jerome crossed swiftly to the remaining cages and unlatched them all. The animals leaped to their freedom. Welles had succeeded with his recapture, however, and had the protesting monkey in his grip, about to deliver the panacea. Jerome made toward him.

"Let it be," he yelled.

Welles pressed the hypodermic into the monkey's body, but before he could depress the plunger Jerome had pulled at his wrist. The hypodermic spat its poison into the air and then fell to the ground. The monkey, wresting itself free, followed.

Jerome pulled Welles close. "I told you to *let it be,*" he said.

Welles's response was to drive his fist into Jerome's wounded flank. Tears of pain spurted from his eyes, but he didn't release the doctor. The stimulus, unpleasant as it was, could not dissuade him from holding that beating heart close. He wished, embracing Welles like a prodigal, that he could ignite himself, that the dream of burning flesh he had endured would now become a reality, consuming maker and made in one cleansing flame. But his flesh was only flesh; his bone, bone. What miracles he had seen had been a private revelation, and now there was no time to communicate their glories or their horrors. What he had seen would die with him, to be rediscovered (perhaps) by some future self, only to be forgotten and discovered again. Like the story of love the radio had told; the same joy lost and found, found and lost. He stared at Welles with new comprehension dawning, hearing still the terrified beat of the man's heart. The doctor was *wrong*. If he left the man to live, he would come to know his error. They were not presagers of the millennium. They had both been dreaming.

"Don't kill me," Welles pleaded. "I don't want to die."

More fool you, Jerome thought, and let the man go.

Welles's bafflement was plain. He couldn't believe that his appeal for life had been answered. Anticipating a blow with every step he took he backed away from Jerome, who simply turned his back on the doctor and walked away.

From downstairs there came a shout, and then many shouts. Police, Welles guessed. They had presumably found the body of the officer who'd been on guard at the door. In moments only they would be coming up the stairs. There was no time now for finishing the tasks he'd come here to perform. He had to be away before they arrived.

On the floor below Carnegie watched the armed officers disappear up the stairs. There was a faint smell of burning in the air. He feared the worst.

I am the man who comes after the act, he thought to himself. I am perpetually upon the scene when the best of the action is over. Used as he was to waiting, patient as a loyal dog, this time he could not hold his anxieties in check while the others went ahead. Disregarding the voices advising him to wait, he began up the stairs.

The laboratory on the top floor was empty but for the monkeys and Johannson's corpse. The toxicologist lay on his face where he had fallen, neck broken. The emergency exit, which let on to the fire escape, was open; smoky air was being sucked out through it. As Carnegie stepped away from Johannson's body officers were already on the fire escape calling to their colleagues below to seek out the fugitive.

"Sir?"

Carnegie looked across at the mustachioed individual who had approached him.

"What is it?"

The officer pointed to the other end of the laboratory, to the test chamber. There was somebody at the window. Carnegie recognized the features, even though they were much changed. It was Jerome. At first he thought the man was watching him, but a short perusal scotched that idea. Jerome was staring, tears on his face, at his own reflection in the smeared glass. Even as Carnegie watched, the face retreated with the gloom of the chamber.

Other officers had noticed the man too. They were moving down the length of the laboratory, taking up positions behind the benches where they had a good line on the door, weapons at the ready. Carnegie had been present in such situations before; they had their own, terrible momentum. Unless he intervened, there would be blood.

"No," he said, "hold your fire."

He pressed the protesting officer aside and began to walk down the laboratory, making no attempt to conceal his advance. He walked past sinks in which the remains of *Blind Boy* guttered, past the bench under which, a short age ago, they'd found the dead Dance. A monkey, its head bowed, dragged itself across his path, apparently deaf to his proximity. He let it find a hole to die in, then moved on to the chamber door. It was ajar. He reached for the handle. Behind him the laboratory had fallen completely silent; all eyes were on him. He pulled the door open. Fingers tightened on triggers. There was no attack however. Carnegie stepped inside.

Jerome was standing against the opposite wall. If he saw Carnegie enter, or heard him, he made no sign of it. A dead monkey lay at his feet, one hand still grasping the hem of his trousers. Another whimpered in the corner, holding its head in its hands.

"Jerome?"

Was it Carnegie's imagination, or could he smell strawberries?

Jerome blinked.

"You're under arrest," Carnegie said. Hendrix would appreciate the irony of that, he thought. The man moved his bloody hand from the stab wound in his side to the front of his trousers and began to stroke himself.

"Too late," Jerome said. He could feel the last fire rising in him. Even if this intruder chose to cross the chamber and arrest him now, the intervening seconds would deny him his capture. *Death was here*. And what

was it, now that he saw it clearly? Just another seduction, another sweet darkness to be filled up, and plea-
sured and made fertile.

A spasm began in his perineum, and lightning traveled in two directions from the spot, up his rod and up
his spine. A laugh began in his throat.

In the corner of the chamber the monkey, hearing
Jerome's humor, began to whimper again. The sound
momentarily claimed Carnegie's attention, and when his
gaze flitted back to Jerome the short-sighted eyes had
closed, the hand had dropped, and he was dead, standing against the wall. For a short time the body defied
gravity. Then, gracefully the legs buckled and Jerome
fell forward. He was, Carnegie saw, a sack of bones, no
more. It was a wonder the man had lived so long.

Cautiously, he crossed to the body and put his finger
to the man's neck. There was no pulse. The remnants of
Jerome's last laugh remained on his face, however, re-
fusing to decay.

"Tell me . . ." Carnegie whispered to the man, sensing that despite his preemption he had missed the moment; that once again he was, and perhaps would
always be, merely a witness of consequences. "Tell me.
What was the joke?"

But the blind boy, as is the wont of his clan, wasn't
telling.

Here is an excerpt from Clive Barker's epic adventure of the imagination, *WEAVEWORLD*.

WEAVEWORLD
by
Clive Barker

I · Homing

1

Nothing ever begins.

There is no first moment, no single word or place from which this or any other story springs.

The threads can always be traced back to some earlier tale, and to the tales that preceded that; though as the narrator's voice recedes the connections will seem to grow more tenuous, for each age will want the tale told as if it were of its own making.

Thus the pagan may be sanctified, the tragic become laughable; great lovers will stoop to sentiment, and demons dwindle to clockwork toys.

Nothing is fixed. In and out the shuttle goes, fact and fiction, mind and matter, woven into patterns that may have only this in common: that hidden amongst them is a filigree which with time will become a world.

It must be arbitrary then, the place at which we choose to embark.

Somewhere between a past half forgotten and a future as yet only glimpsed. This place, for instance.

This garden, untended since the death of its protector three months ago, and now running riot beneath a blindingly bright late August sky; its fruits hanging unharvested, its herbaceous borders coaxed to mutiny by a summer of torrential rain and sudden, sweltering days.

This house, identical to the hundreds of others in this street alone, built with its back so close to the railway track that the passage of the slow train from Liverpool to Crewe rocks the china dogs on the dining-room windowsill.

And with this young man, who now steps out of the back door and makes his way down the beleaguered path to a ramshackle hut from which there rises a welcoming chorus of coos and flutterings.

His name is Calhoun Mooney, but he's universally known as Cal. He is twenty-six, and has worked for five years at an insurance firm in the city center. It's a job he takes no pleasure in, but escape from the city he's lived in all his life seems more unlikely than ever since the death of his mother, all of which may account for the weary expression on his well-made face.

He approaches the door of the pigeon loft, opens it, and at that moment—for want of a better—this story takes wing.

2

Cal had told his father several times that the wood at the bottom of the loft door was deteriorating. It could only be a matter of time before the planks rotted completely, giving the rats who lived and grew gross along the railway line access to the pigeons. But Brendan Mooney had shown little or no interest in his racing birds since Eileen's death. This despite, or perhaps because, the birds had been his abiding passion during her life. How often had Cal heard his mother complain that Brendan spent more time with his precious pigeons than he did inside the house?

She would not have had that complaint to make now; now Cal's father sat most of every day at the back window staring out into the garden and watching the wilderness steadily taking charge of his wife's handiwork, as if he might find in the spectacle of dissolution some clue as to how his grief might be similarly erased. There was little sign that he was learning much from his vigil, however. Every day, when Cal came back to the house in Chariot Street—a house he thought to have left for good half a decade ago, but which his father's isolation had obliged him to return to—it seemed he found Brendan slightly smaller. Not hunched, but somehow *shrunken*, as though he'd decided to present the smallest possible target to a world suddenly grown hostile.

Murmuring a welcome to the forty or so birds in the loft, Cal stepped inside, to be met with a scene of high agitation. All but a few of the pigeons were flying back and forth in their cages, near to hysteria. Had the rats been in, Cal wondered?

He cast around for any damage, but there was no visible sign of what had fueled this furor.

He'd never seen them so excited. For fully half a minute he stood in bewilderment watching their display, the din of their wings making his head reel, before deciding to step into the largest of the cages and claim the prize birds from the mêlée before they did themselves damage.

He unlatched the cage, and had opened it no more than two or three inches when one of last year's champions, a normally sedate cock known, as were they all, by his number——33—— flew at the gap. Shocked by the speed of the bird's approach, Cal let the door go, and in the seconds between his fingers' slipping from the latch and his retrieval of it, 33 was out.

"Damn you!" Cal shouted, cursing himself as much as the bird, for he'd left the door of the loft itself ajar, and——apparently careless of what harm he might do to himself in his bid——33 was making for the sky.

In the few moments it took Cal to latch the cage again, the bird was through the door and away. Cal went in stumbling pursuit, but by the time he got back into the open air, 33 was already fluttering up above the garden. At roof height he flew around in three ever larger circles, as if orienting himself. Then he seemed to fix his objective and took off in a north-northeasterly direction.

A rapping drew Cal's attention, and he looked down to see his father standing at the window, mouthing something to him. There was more animation on Brendan's harried face than Cal had seen in months; the escape of the bird seemed to have temporarily roused him from his despondency. Moments later he was at the back door, asking what had happened. Cal had no time for explanations.

"It's off," he yelled.

Then, keeping his eye on the sky as he went, he started down the path at the side of the house.

When he reached the front the bird was still in sight. Cal leapt the fence and crossed Chariot Street at a run, determined to give chase. It was, he knew, an all but hopeless pursuit. With a tail wind a prime bird could reach a top speed of seventy miles an hour, and though 33 had not raced for the best part of a year he could still easily outpace a human runner. But Cal knew he couldn't go back to his father without making some effort to track the escapee, however futile.

At the bottom of the street he lost sight of his quarry behind the rooftops, and so made a detour to the footbridge that crossed the Woolton road, mounting the steps three and four at a time. From the top he was rewarded with a good view of the city. North towards Woolton Hill, and off east, and southeast, over Allerton towards Hunt's Cross. Row upon row of council-house roofs presented themselves, shimmering in the fierce heat of the afternoon, the herringbone rhythm of the closed-parked streets rapidly giving way to the industrial wastelands of Speke.

Cal could see the pigeon too, though it was a rapidly diminishing dot.

It mattered little, for from this elevation 33's destination was perfectly apparent. Less than two miles from the bridge the air was full of wheeling birds, drawn to the spot no doubt by some concentration of food in the area. Every year brought at least one such day, when the ant or gnat population suddenly boomed, and the bird life of the city was united in its gluttony. Gulls up from the mud banks of the Mersey, flying tip to tip with thrush and jackdaw and starting, all content to join the jamboree while the summer still warmed their backs.

This, no doubt, was the call 33 had heard. Bored with his balanced diet of maize and maple peas, tired of the pecking order of the loft and the predictability of each day, the bird had wanted out; wanted up and away. A day of high life, of food that had to be chased a little, and tasted all the better for that; of the companionship of wild things. All this went through Cal's head, in a vague sort of way, while he watched the circling flocks.

It would be perfectly impossible, he knew, to locate an individual bird amongst these riotous thousands. He would have to trust that 33 would be content with his feast on the wing and, when he was sated, do as he was trained to do and come home. Nevertheless, the sheer spectacle of so many birds exercised a peculiar fascination, and crossing the bridge, Cal began to make his way towards the epicenter of this feathered cyclone.

II · Who Moved the Ground?

1

he birds did not stop their spiraling over the city as Cal
proached. For every one that flew off, another three or four
ined the throng.

The phenomenon had not gone unnoticed. People stood on
e pavement and on doorsteps, hands shading their eyes from
e glare of the sky, and stared heavenwards. Opinions were
erywhere ventured as to the reason for this congregation.
al didn't stop to offer his, but threaded his way through the
aze of streets, on occasion having to double back and find a
w route but by degrees getting closer to the hub.

And now, as he approached, it became apparent that his
st theory had been incorrect. The birds were not feeding.
here was no swooping nor squabbling over a six-legged
umb, nor any sign in the lower air of the insect life that
ight have attracted these numbers. The birds were simply
rcling. Some of the smaller species, sparrows and finches,
d tired of flying and now lined rooftops and fences, leaving
eir larger brethren—carrion-crows, magpies, gulls—to oc-
py the heights. There was no scarcity of pigeons here either;
e wild variety banking and wheeling in flocks of fifty or
ore, their shadows rippling across the rooftops. There were
me domesticated birds too, doubtless escapees like 33. Ca-
ries and budgerigars: birds called from their millet and their
lls by whatever force had summoned the others. For these
rds, being here was effectively suicide. Though their fellows
ere at present too excited by this ritual to take note of the
ts in their midst, they would not be so indifferent when the
rcling spell no longer bound them. They would be cruel and
ick. They'd fall on the canaries and the budgerigars and
ck out their eyes, killing them for the crime of being tamed.

But for now, the parliament was at peace. It mounted the
r, higher, ever higher, busying the sky.

The pursuit of this spectacle had led Cal to a part of the city he'd seldom explored. Here the plain square houses of the council estates gave way to a forlorn and eerie no-man's-land where streets of once-fine three-storey terraced houses still stood, inexplicably preserved from the bulldozer, surrounded by areas leveled in expectation of a boom-time that had never come; islands in a dust sea.

It was one of these streets—*Rue Street* the sign read—that seemed the point over which the flocks were focused. There were more sizable assemblies of exhausted birds here than any of the adjacent streets; they twittered and preened themselves on the eaves and chimney tops and television aerials.

Cal scanned sky and roof alike, making his way along Rue Street as he did so. And there—a thousand-to-one chance—he caught sight of his bird. A solitary pigeon, dividing a cloud of sparrows. Years of watching the sky, waiting for pigeons return from races, had given him an eagle eye; he could recognize a particular bird by a dozen idiosyncracies in its flight pattern. He had found 33; no doubt of it. But even as he watched, the bird disappeared behind the roofs of Rue Street.

He gave chase afresh, finding a narrow alley which cut between the terraced houses halfway along the road and let out onto the larger alley that ran behind the row. It had not been well kept. Piles of household refuse had been dumped along its length; orphan dustbins overturned, their contents scattered.

But twenty yards from where he stood, there was work going on. Two removal men were maneuvering an armchair out of the yard behind one of the houses, while a third stared up at the birds. Several hundred were assembled on the yard walls, window sills and railings. Cal wandered along the alley scrutinizing this assembly for pigeons. He found a dozen or more amongst the multitude, but not the one he sought.

"What d'you make of it?"

He had come within ten yards of the removal men, and one of them, the idler, was addressing the question to him.

"I don't know," he answered honestly.

"Maybe they're goin' to migrate," said the younger of the two armchair carriers, letting drop his half of the burden and staring up at the sky.

"Don't be an idiot, Shane," said the other man, a West Indian. His name—Gideon—was emblazoned on the back of

overalls. "Why'd they migrate in the middle of the fuckin'
ummer?"

"Too hot," was the idler's reply. "That's what it is. Too
ckin' hot. It's cooking' their brains up there."

Gideon had now put down his half of the armchair and was
uning against the back-yard wall, applying a flame to the
lf-spent cigarette he'd fished from his top pocket.
Vouldn't be bad, would it?" he mused, "being a bird. Gettin'
r end away all spring, then fuckin' off to the South of
ance as soon as yer get a chill on yer bollocks."

"They don't live long," said Cal.

"Do they not?" said Gideon, drawing on his cigarette. He
rugged. "Short and sweet," he said. "That'd suit me."

Shane plucked at the half-dozen blond hairs of his would-
moustache. "Yer know somethin' about birds, do yer?" he
id to Cal.

"Only pigeons."

"Race 'em, do you?"

"Once in a while—"

"Me brother-in-law keeps whippets," said the third man,
e idler. He looked at Cal as though this coincidence verged
the miraculous, and would now fuel hours of debate. But
Cal could think of to say was:

"Dogs."

"That's right," said the other man, delighted that they were
one accord on the issue. "He's got five. Only one died."

"Pity," said Cal.

"Not really. It was fuckin' blind in one eye and couldn't
e in the other."

The man guffawed at this observation, which promptly
ought the exchange to a dead halt. Cal turned his attention
ck to the birds, and he grinned to see—there on the upper
indow-ledge of the house—*his* bird.

"I see him," he said.

Gideon followed his gaze. "What's that, then?"

"My pigeon. He escaped." Cal pointed. "There. In the
iddle of the sill. See him?"

All three now looked.

"Worth something, is he?" said the idler.

"Trust you, Bazo," Shane commented.

"Just asking," Bazo replied.

"He's won prizes," said Cal, with some pride. He was

keeping his eyes glued to 33, but the pigeon showed no sig
of wanting to fly; he just preened his wing feathers, and on
in a while turned a beady eye up to the sky.

"Stay there . . ." Cal told the bird, under his breatl
". . . don't move." Then, to Gideon: "Is it all right if I go i
Try and catch him?"

"Help yourself. The auld girl who had the house's be
carted off the hospital. We're taking the furniture to pay h
bills. Not that there's much left worth selling."

Cal ducked through into the yard, negotiating the bric-
brac the trio had dumped there, and went into the house.

It was a shambles inside. If the occupant had ever own
anything of substance it had long since been removed. Tl
few pictures still hanging were worthless; the furniture w
old, but not old enough to have come back into fashion; tl
rugs, cushions and curtains so aged they were fit only for tl
incinerator. The walls and ceiling were stained by many year
accrual of smoke, its source the candles that sat on every she
and sill, stalactites of yellowed wax depending from them.

He made his way through the warren of pokey, dark room
and through into the hallway. The scene was just as dispiriti
here. The brown linoleum was rucked up and torn, and ever
where there was the pervasive smell of must and dust a
creeping rot. She was well out of this squalid place, C
thought, wherever she was; better off in a hospital, where
least the sheets were dry.

He began to climb the stairs. It was a curious sensatio
ascending into the murk of the upper storey, becoming blind
stair by stair, with the sound of birds scurrying across the slat
above his skull, and beyond that the muted cries of gull a
crow. Though it was no doubt self-deception, he seemed to he
their voices *circling*, as though this very place were the center
their attentions. An image appeared in his head, of a photogra
from *National Geographic*. A study of stars, taken with a slo
release camera, the pin-point lights describing circles as the
moved, or appeared to move, across the sky, with the Pole Sta
the Nail of Heaven, steady in their midst.

The wheeling sound, and the picture it evoked, began
dizzy him. He suddenly felt weak, even afraid.

This was no time for such frailities, he chided himself. I
had to claim the bird before it flew off again. He picked up h
pace. At the top of the stairs he maneuvered past several iten

of bedroom furniture, and opened one of the several doors that he was presented with. The room he had chosen was adjacent to the one whose sill 33 occupied. Sun streamed through the curtainless window; the stale heat brought fresh sweat to his brow. The room had been emptied of furniture, the only souvenir of occupancy a calendar for the year 1961. On it was a photograph of a lion beneath a tree, its shaggy, monolithic head laid on vast paws, its gaze contemplative.

Cal went out onto the landing again, selected another door and was this time delivered into the right room. There, beyond the grimy glass, was the pigeon.

Now it was all a question of tactics. He had to be careful not to startle the bird. He approached the window cautiously. On the sun-drenched sill, 33 cocked its head and blinked its eye, but made no move. Cal held his breath and put his hands on the frame to haul the window up, but there was no budging it. A quick perusal showed why. The frame had been sealed up shut years ago, a dozen or more nails driven deep into the wood. A primitive form of crime prevention, but no doubt reassuring to an old woman living alone.

From the yard below, he heard Gideon's voice. Peering down, he could just see the trio dragging a large rolled-up carpet out of the house, Gideon giving orders in a ceaseless stream.

"—to my left, Bazo. *Left!* Don't you know which is your left?"

"I'm going left."

"Not *your* left, yer idiot. *My* left."

The bird on the sill was undisturbed by this commotion. It seemed quite happy on its perch.

Cal headed back downstairs, deciding as he went that the only option remaining was to climb up onto the yard wall and see if he couldn't coax the bird down from there. He cursed himself for not having brought a pocketful of grain. Coos and sweet words would just have to do.

By the time he stepped out into the heat of the yard once more, the removal men had successfully manhandled the carpet out of the house, and were taking a rest after their exertions.

"No luck?" said Shane, seeing Cal emerge.

"The window won't budge. I'll have to try from down here."

He caught a deprecating look from Bazo. "You'll never reach the bugger from here," the man said, scratching the expanse of beer-gut that gleamed between T-shirt hem and belt.

"I'll try from the wall," said Cal.

"Watch yerself—" Gideon said.

"Thanks."

"—You could break back—"

Using pits in the crumbling mortar for footholds, Cal hauled himself up onto the eight-foot wall that divided this yard from its neighbor.

The sun was hot on his neck and the top of his head, and something of the giddiness he'd experienced climbing the stairs returned. He straddled the wall as though it were a horse, until he got used to the height. Though the perch was the width of a brick, and offered ample enough walking space, heights and he had never been happy companions.

"Looks like it's been a nice piece of handiwork," said Gideon, in the yard below. Cal glanced down, and saw that the West Indian was now on his haunches beside the carpet, which he'd rolled out far enough to expose an elaborately woven border.

Bazo wandered over to where Gideon crouched, and srutinized the property. He was balding, Cal could see, his hair scrupulously pasted down with oil to conceal the spot.

"Pity it's not in better nick," said Shane.

"Hold yer horses," said Bazo. "Let's have a better look."

Cal returned his attention to the problem of standing upright. At least the carpet would divert his audience for a few moments—long enough, he prayed, for him to get to his feet. There was no breath of wind here to alleviate the fury of the sun; he could feel sweat trickle down his torso and glue his underwear to his buttocks. Gingerly, he started to stand, bringing one leg up into a kneeling position, both hands clinging to the brick like grim death.

From below, there were murmurs of approval as more of the carpet was exposed to the light.

"Look at the work in that," said Gideon.

"Are you thinking what I'm thinkin'?" said Bazo, his voice lowered.

"I don't know till you tell me," came Gideon's reply.

"What say we take it down to Gilchrist's? We might get a price for this."

"The Chief'll know it's gone," Shane protested.

"Keep it down," said Bazo, quietly reminding his companions of Cal's presence. In fact Cal was far too concerned with his inept tightrope act to bother himself with their petty theft. He had finally got the soles of both feet up on the top of the wall, and was about to try standing up.

In the yard, the conversation went on.

"Take the far end, Shane, let's have a look at the whole thing. . . . "

"D'you think it's Persian?"

"Haven't a fuckin' clue."

Very slowly, Cal stood upright, his arms extended at ninety degrees from his body. Feeling as stable as he was ever going to feel, he chanced a quick look up at the window sill. The bird was still there.

From below he heard the sound of the carpet being unrolled further, the men's grunts punctuated with words of admiration.

Ignoring their presence as best he could, he took his first faltering step along the wall.

"Hey there . . ." he murmured up to the escapee. ". . . Remember me?"

Thirty-three took no notice. Cal advanced a second trembling step, and a third, his confidence growing. He was getting the trick of this balancing business now.

"Come on down," he coaxed, a prosaic Romeo.

The bird finally seemed to recognize his owner's voice, and cocked his head in Cal's direction.

"Here, boy . . ." Cal said, tentatively raising his hand towards the window as he risked another step.

At that instant, either his foot slipped or the brick gave way beneath his heel. He heard himself loose a cry of alarm, which panicked the birds lining the sill. They were up and off, their wing-beats ironic applause, as he flailed on the wall. His panicked gaze went first to his feet, then to the yard below.

No, not the yard; that had disappeared. It was the carpet he saw. It had been entirely unrolled, and it filled the yard from wall to wall.

What happened next occupied mere seconds, but either his

mind was lightning fast, or the moments played truant, for it seemed he had all the time he needed. . . .

Time to appreciate the startling intricacy of the design laid out beneath him; an awesome proliferation of exquisitely executed detail. Age had bled brightness from the colors of the weave, mellowing vermilion to rose, and cobalt to a chalky blue; and here and there the carpet had become threadbare, but from where Cal teetered the effect was still overwhelming. Every inch of the carpet was worked with motif. Even the border brimmed with designs, all subtly different from their neighbors. The effect was not over-busy; every detail was clear to Cal's feasting eyes. In one place a dozen motifs congregated as if banded together; in another, they stood apart like rival siblings. Some kept their station along the border; others spilled into the main field, as if eager to join the teeming throng there.

In the field itself ribbons of color described arabesques across a background of sultry browns and greens, forms that were pure abstraction—bright jottings from some wild man's diary—jostling with stylized flora and fauna. But this complexity paled beside the centerpiece of the carpet: a huge medallion, its colors as various as a summer garden, into which a hundred subtle geometrics had been cunningly woven, so that the eye could read each pattern as flower or theorem, order or turmoil, and find each choice echoed somewhere in the grand design.

He saw all of this in one prodigious glance. In this second, the vision laid before him began to change.

From the corner of his eye he registered that the rest of the world—the yard, and the men who occupied it, the houses, the wall he'd been toppling from—all were winking out of existence. Suddenly he was hanging in the air, the carpet vaster by the moment beneath him, its glorious configurations filling his head.

The design was shifting, he saw. The knots were restless, trembling to stilt themselves, and the colors seemed to be merging into each other, new forms springing from this marriage of dyes.

Implausible as it seemed, the carpet was coming to life.

A landscape—or rather a confusion of landscapes thrown together in fabulous disarray—was emerging from the warp and the weft. Was that not a mountain he could see below him, pressing its head up through a cloud of color? And was that not a river, and could he not hear its roar as it fell in white-water torrents into a shadowed gorge?

There was a *world* below him.

And he was suddenly a bird, a wingless bird hovering for a breathless instant on a balmy, sweet-scented wind, sole witness to the miracle sleeping below.

There was more to claim his eye with every thump of his heart.

A lake with myriad islands dotting its placid waters like breaching whales. A dappled quilt of fields, their grasses and grains swept by the same tides of air that kept him aloft. Velvet woodland creeping up the sleek flank of a hill on whose pinnacle a watchtower perched, sun and cloud-shadow drifting across its white walls.

There were other signs of habitation too, though nothing of the people themselves. A cluster of dwellings hugging a river-bend; several houses beetling along the edge of a cliff, tempting gravity. And a town too, laid out in a city-planner's nightmare, half its streets hopelessly serpentine, the other half cul-de-sacs.

The same casual indifference to organization was evident everywhere. He saw zones temperate and intemperate, fruitful and barren, thrown together in defiance of all laws geological or climatic, as if by a God whose taste was for contradiction.

How fine it would be to walk there, he thought, with so much variety pressed into so little space, not knowing whether turning the next corner would bring ice or fire. Such complexity was beyond the wit of a cartographer. To be there, in that world, would be to live a perpetual adventure.

And at the center of this burgeoning province, perhaps the most awesome sight of all: a mass of slate-colored cloud, the innards of which were in perpetual, spiraling motion. The sight reminded him of the birds wheeling above the house in Rue Street—an echo of this greater wheel.

At the thought of them, and the place he'd left behind, he heard their voices—and in that moment the wind that had swept him up from the world below, keeping him aloft, faltered.

He felt the horror in his stomach first, and then his bowels: he was going to fall.

The tumult of the birds grew louder, crowing their delight

at his descent. He, the usurper of their element; he, who h
snatched a glimpse of a miracle, would now be dashed
death upon it.

He started to yell, but the speed of his fall stole the c
from his tongue. The air roared in his ears and tore at his ha
He tried to spread his arms to slow his descent but the attem
instead threw him head over heels and over again, until he
longer knew earth from sky. There was some mercy in this,
dimly thought. At least he'd been blind to death's proximi
Just tumbling and tumbling until—

—the world went out.

He fell through a darkness unrelieved by stars, the bir
still loud in his ears, and hit the ground, hard.

It hurt, and went on hurting, which struck him as od
Oblivion, he'd always assumed, would be a painless con
tion. And soundless too. But there were voices.

"Say something . . ." one of them demanded, ". . . if i
only goodbye."

There was laughter now.

He opened his eyes a hair's breadth. The sun was blin
ingly bright, until Gideon's bulk eclipsed it.

"Have you broken anything?" the man wanted to know.

Cal opened his eyes a fraction wider.

"Say something, will you?"

He raised his head a few inches, and looked about him.
was lying in the yard, on the carpet.

"What happened?"

"You fell off the wall," said Shane.

"Must have missed your footing," Gideon suggested.

"Fell," Cal said, pulling himself up into a sitting positio
He felt nauseous.

"Don't think you've done much damage," said Gideon.
few scrapes, that's all.

Cal looked down at himself, verifying the man's remar
He'd taken skin off his right arm from wrist to elbow, a
there was tenderness down his body where he'd hit t
ground, but there were no sharp pains. The only real har
was to his dignity, and that was seldom fatal.

He got to his feet, wincing, eyes to the ground. The wea
was playing dumb. There was no tell-tale tremor in the ro
of knots, no sign that hidden heights and depths were about
make themselves known. Nor was there any sign from t

others that they'd seen anything miraculous. To all intents and purposes the carpet beneath his feet was simply that: a carpet.

He hobbled towards the yard gate, offering a muttered thanks to Gideon. As he stepped out into the alley, Bazo said:

"Yer bird flew off."

Cal gave a small shrug and went on his way.

What had he just experienced? A hallucination, brought on by too much sun or too little breakfast. If so, it had been startlingly real. He looked up at the birds, still circling overhead. *They* sensed something untoward here too; that was why they'd gathered. Either that, or they and he were sharing the same delusion.

All, in sum, that he could be certain of was his bruising. That, and the fact that though he was standing no more than two miles from his father's house, in the city in which he'd spent his entire life, he felt as homesick as a lost child.

"I have seen the future of horror, and its name is Clive Barker."

–Stephen King

CLIVE BARKER

Master of horror, Clive Barker has thrilled countless readers with his bizarre and terrifying short story collections, *THE INHUMAN CONDITION* and *IN THE FLESH*.

Now, Barker brings us *WEAVEWORLD*, his most visionary horror novel yet—a prosaic liverpool clerk falls into a magic carpet and enters the cursed and enchanted Weaveworld of the Seerkind.

☐ WEAVEWORLD .... 66506/$4.95

☐ IN THE FLESH .... 61270/$3.95

☐ THE INHUMAN
   CONDITION .... 68463/$4.50